I lay on the red shag
and filled a pipe
minutes Donr
arched her b
Then she lay

'I can't mak　　　　　　　. 'I just
thought it would　　　　　　ow, friendly,
if you saw me wit　　　　　once before the
end of the summer.

She stood up and slowly peeled off her pants
and blouse and brassiere and panties. She had
an excellent body. If she could let go, she would
be one of the most sensuous women in the world.

'Close your eyes,' she said.

The next sensation was that of her hand in a
mink glove, rubbing my genitals . . .

THE SALINE SOLUTION

Marco Vassi

First published in Great Britain in 1991
by Nexus Books
332 Ladbroke Grove
London W10 5AH
Reprinted 1992, 1994

First published in 1989
Copyright © Marco Vassi 1971

Typeset by Avocet Robinson, Buckingham
Printed in Great Britain by
Cox & Wyman Ltd, Reading, Berks.

ISBN 0 352 32429 5

This book is dedicated to the Sun

This book is a work of fiction.
In real life, make sure you practise safe sex.

You should know that I destroy nothing:
I record, I record the *imminent*,
the thirst of a world which is
canceling itself out and which,
upon the wreck of its appearances,
races toward the unknown and the immeasurable,
toward a spasmodic style.

E.M. Cioran

It is that which you see before you –
begin to reason about it
and you at once fall into error.

Huang Po

I

We didn't know whether we wanted the baby, so we drifted in indecision until Lucinda passed the third month of pregnancy. And then it became a question of murder.

It was to have been a casual affair of impersonal intensity. We played at all the slick chic city games that New York tosses to its corroded citizens as it attempts to raise the final pockmarked erection on the deathbed of western civilisation. We began with boredom and openly oblique glances at one another's bodies, estimating the size of the cock and the texture of the breasts as we brought the tips of our tongues to our teeth and hummed reflectively. We both had an unencumbered summer before us, and were thinking what a pleasure it would be to have a bedmate for the season, someone sophisticated, someone who would curl up and fall away easily when the leaves began to turn in the autumn. With decadent delicacy we mounted a scene which we could play like real life on an actual planet in the universe and that had the brass balls to exist and manifest itself in utterly arbitrary format. We decided to spend the summer on Fire Island.

But she was empty, and still sought to be fulfilled. And

I overflowed with conflict, and had fantasies of peace. Thus the second time we fucked I entered her from behind and drove so compactly into her need that I dislodged the diaphragm and sent my sperm scurrying into her womb. Our bodies froze, her arse raised and tilted, her cunt glued to my cock, and there was not a tremor anywhere inside us, only the consciousness of that single messenger braving its way through fallopian mazes and immeasurable canyons to liberate the living awareness of another human entity from its protein meditation. The child was conceived.

And then the hatred began, for Lucinda and I had become implicated in birth, and were half in love with death, because we could both hear the siren song to the species. Suicide had become our collective destiny, and those who honoured life would be left like erratic lunatics to wonder at their choice while the rest of manwomankind marched its mindless progress towards destruction. As the autumn approached, our decision became clearer. Abortion had just become legal, and we wondered whether it had also become admirable.

Lucinda opened the door of the apartment. We were spending a weekend in the city, away from the heavy presence of the ocean with its constant vast indifference to the arrogant creature which had begun in the scummy film on its surface and now littered its shores with all forms of waste. I lay back on the bed, the taste of sperm still stinging my tongue. In the thrilling semi-concealment of a clump of bushes in Central Park, I had knelt with the rough corduroy against my cheeks, the cold white zipper catching at my lips, and the hard intimate cock romping in my mouth like a porpoise at play. The man who had stood over me was a stranger, someone whose eyes had met mine in that unmistakable glance which passes between men who desire one another's bodies. There was no passion or personality in my behaviour, merely a muted impulse which I had long ago ceased to question and which led me again and again into this classic pose of cocksucker. His legs trembled as he began to come, and I held his arse in my hands, drawing him more deeply into my mouth. He sucked the breath through his teeth, grabbed my shoulders, and came without any stinginess or reserve, his ejaculation squirting into my throat.

While I cruised among the benches and the bushes, Lucinda went to visit her mother. I didn't tell her about these adventures of mine because we had made an agreement not to test one another's limits of acceptance or jealousy. But when I returned to the apartment, I was horny; I wanted to have done to me what I had just done for another.

She threw off her cape and dropped her handbag on the floor. It was a yellow leather pouch, richly embroidered with violet wool and bits of glass, made in Portugal. It was expensive enough to transform its gaudiness into good taste. She looked at me from across the room, and without a word we exchanged descriptions of our moods. We both wanted to fuck; we both wanted privacy. She went into the bathroom to undress, leaving the door half open. As she removed her bra, her dark breasts sagged with a pendulous grace that never ceased to be seductive. I was no longer excited just seeing her body, as I am the first few times with a woman. Gross visual curiosity is very quickly satisfied. Now I had to couple what I saw with an eagerness to touch in order to be aroused.

'I ran into Albert today,' she said, her back to me. 'He's let his hair grow and is wearing clear polish on his nails. I think he's finally admitting to people that he's gay.'

'It's about time,' I said. 'He's almost fifty.'

'He said that Tiny Tim is really William F. Buckley in drag.'

I laughed, but I could feel the energy flowing out of me and into that silent pit of depression which formed the core of her being. I felt my cock stir. The quality of eternal suffering, of bottomless helplessness, was the essential aspect of her erotic appeal. To fuck her was to take a final revenge for the evil which existed in the world. I bridled at my desire. Part of me wanted to yield, to drown in the black numbness of her centre. And some of me fought desperately against the pull, attempting to retain what thin thread of moral sensibility still ran through my calculations.

'This is playing games with personality constructs,' I thought. 'Just fuck her, use her as she needs to be used. There is no abstract decency, there is only the pulse of survival, and it knows no other dictate than cruelty. There is only what we are, not what we think we should be.'

I split internally into warring ideological camps, the many identities battling for supremacy. All the conflicting conditionings of my entire life clamoured in contradiction. 'What does it mean any more, to be human?' I wondered.

Two nights earlier I had lain next to her, my hand on her belly, feeling the life force swell and diminish with each breath. 'We are all transformers,' I thought, 'Just oxygen pumps, one rusted link in the chain of sentient beings. All of our ideas and visions and speculations on the matter are only illusion.'

I had felt totally alone, caught in the ineluctability of my own death. 'It won't be any big deal,' I thought. 'No extra added significance. My heart will stop. And I won't be.'

On the level of ego, the realisation had horrified me. But as I found myself rising to terms with the fact of nonexistence as an objective reality which constantly mocks all that is, I retreated into a state of warm irony.

Lucinda came out of the bathroom. She was naked. For an instant her body seemed to glow and surge forward, her nipples radiating and cunt gaping like the mouth of a landed fish. The conflict between the simple animal urge to plunge my cock into her cunt, and the storm of thought thundering in my head, paralysed me, and I made no sign

14

for her to join me on the bed.

'Are you hungry?' she said. I nodded.

She made one of those deceptively simple meals that belie the years of experience in cooking that most women accumulate from childhood. It had rice and vegetables and came with pieces of home-baked bread and tea. It was coherent, and made a single impression as a dish, an effect I could never achieve when I cooked. We gossiped as we ate, finding in that particular form of tender maliciousness the proper quality of energy to aid in digestion of food. Lucinda was thirty-five. I was two years younger.

We had good fucking, good food, and a non-intrusive intellectual rapport. But our emotions died from lack of air. The very bonds which form the ground in which the relationship grows can petrify and strangle all future development. And then the couple disbands or continues in some empty reflexive dance with all the essential questions entombed forever. I had seen it so many times, the smug couples who have made all their secret agreements and then use their compromise as a shield. They achieve a deft pseudo-solution to their problems by building and maintaining their life rafts, totally ignoring the holocaust they paddle in.

We fell into silence over tea; we lit cigarettes. I knew that she was locked inside her thoughts, as I was in mine. I thought of the Zen precept, that the only transmission of Mind can be from mind to mind. In the secret movie theatre of my thoughts, the Self appeared, dressed as the last gunfighter in town, looking for a duel to reassure himself of his existence. 'Is anybody else here?' he shouted. Only the ghosts showed their faces from behind the cracked windows which lined the deserted street of the old town. I was nothing but a cacophony of memories, and the thought of real human relationship seemed to have only the dimensions of a daydream.

She took the dishes into the kitchen, and I lay back down

on the bed. She came into the bedroom and lay down next to me, stretching full out on her stomach. Her hair covered her face, and only the nude impersonal expanse of flesh that now was her body spoke to me. I ran my hand from her shoulders to her arse, stroking lightly, feeling the fine prickle of electricity as skin excited skin. She opened her legs a bare inch, just enough to indicate her invitation. There was no pretence of affection.

I lowered myself onto her. All the bulges down the front of me found hollows along her back to nestle in. My knees into the backs of her knees, her buttocks into my groin, my belly into the small of her back, my chest on her spine. I reached under her and worked one breast into each of my hands, feeling the thick pleasure of the soft glandular pressure of her tits. I relaxed my full weight on her and we tacitly abandoned ourselves to the exclusivity of one another's satisfaction. It was as though fucking were a truce, a spacetime in which we could allay alienation and find a temporary comfort in the union of our physical communication. In fucking, the language is basic, the dualities are clear: yes, no; brutal, tender; in, out; agression, passivity; and on down the entire ontology of experience. In fucking, the play of mood captures at least the form, if not the essence, of an extended gesture, which subsumes music, incorporates dance, and attains to poetry.

I let my limp cock fall past the lowest bulge of her buttocks. The tip of it nuzzled the edge of her cunt lips. Her hair tickled my skin. I slid my hands down the front of her, over the cave of her ribcage and her vulnerable stomach, catching the bulge of her in my palms, and began to play at her cunt with my fingers, scratching and pressing at the sensitive folds. Then I slipped one finger into where the wetness began, and she gasped down the entire length of her body. My cock hardened.

I put my fingers under the shaft and pressed it against the whole slit of cunt. My pelvis began to rock, forcing

16

my prick to slide as it grew larger between my hands and the hot deep opening between her legs. So many times, when I was younger, I would be embarrassed at this moment because I hadn't achieved an instant erection, and that feeling would short-circuit any chance of success. But I learned in time that there are few things more erotic for a woman than to feel the process whereby a man gets hard, and to have her cunt gently pried apart with one hand while a cock is guided in with the other.

She moaned once and I felt myself become completely stiff. I was now pushing my cock against her clitoris, inflaming and teasing her. She started to move, trying to capture the head of my cock with her cunt. I became elusive, and the game was on. 'Please,' she said, 'please fuck me.' The poverty of the dialogue found its complement in the richness of the sensations we were feeling. Also, she knew that I frustrated her only in order to allow her to build to higher levels of energy. She moved her arse into me with shameless supplication, and I grew giddy with the waves of heat that coursed through me, melting all my postures and images. And when I could stand the tension no longer, her cunt found me and I sank into her with a loud cry of pleasurepain, and began to swim in the hot and thick and delicious recesses of her body.

She came up on her knees and stretched her torso out, her arms reaching ahead of her, offering her exposed centre to me, to fuck at my own rhythm and speed. She was content to remain still and let the sensations wash over her. I rode her for almost an hour, going through dozens of changes, sometimes smashing brutally into her, and then just letting the tip of my cock gently nudge the edges of her inner lips; or swinging from side to side in erratic patterns, and then lying quietly, feeling my organ throb in her depths like a submarine in a grotto listening for echoes. I pumped into her with even strokes, like a carpenter sawing wood, and exploded into her like an epileptic having a fit; I rose up and hit into her at a sharp downward angle, and then sank down to slip my cock in from underneath and erupt into the roof of her cunt. I fucked the smell of her, and the sight of her, and the possibilities of her. I pushed her down so she lay with her legs together and extended, and sat on her thighs, my knees clasping her arse, and swung into her closed cunt, pulling her buttocks apart, putting my fingers into her arsehole, between her thighs, and around my cock, so that my cock and hands and frenzy all fucked her at once. I put her on her right side and lifted one leg, watching my cock plunge into the great gap which was now all wet hair and trembling heat. She had four orgasms.

And when I got physically tired, and bored with the cycles of excitement and detachment, I had her kneel again as though she were in church praying, and then prostrate herself fully forward from the waist, her spine bent, her belly hanging, her cunt at an angle for deepest penetration, and I let myself spin off into an unobstructed movement, my pelvis shuddering rapidly as I let the energy ripple freely through my body, enjoying the crashing pleasure of the way her cunt caught my cock and held it as I slid in and out of her, and the pose of abject submission she took before me, and I let the sperm bubble through and flush out into her as I yelled in release, a hairy solipsist in the throes of a loveless orgasm.

Gradually she let herself sink full-length on the bed, and I lay on top of her. We were in exactly the same position we had held before we started to fuck. It made everything that had happened in between seem futile. But that also seemed true of life. In all of the times we had had sex, I had never let go in her arms. I always performed, not in the adolescent sense of trying to be the best fuck she ever had, but in the more insidious way of never losing my selfconsciousness. Both in and out of bed I kept my distance, and we shared no existential rushes.

18

Secretly we both played the game of pretending that each of us had the power to save the other from dying.

I suddenly became very aware of the body lying underneath me, of this human being now thinking her thoughts as I was thinking mine, perhaps as aware as I of the gap between us, and wondered whether there were such a thing as love which could erase the essential strangeness of the other. I could imagine myself after forty years looking into Lucinda's eyes and saying, 'I never did know who you were, really.' But of course, that would be no more than I would say to myself. Freud was wrong. The opposite of Eros is not Thanatos, but Absurdity.

We got up and moved randomly around the apartment, and I drifted into the kitchen to make tea, finding a therapeutic calmness in the orderliness of the ritual. 'Let's bring the radio in to the city next time,' Lucinda said.

We had taken all our electronic props to Fire Island, and when we came into the city for a few days we felt like junkies whose supply had been cut off. The thoroughness with which the noise made by the media had permeated our sense of environment was chilling. Once, when Lucinda was bitching about not having the stereo in the city, I launched into a long rap on the value of returning to one's inner resources and she shot back, '*What* inner resources?'

I sipped the tea and looked out the window to the apartment building across the alley. The woman who was lying in bed, whatever time we looked, was still there, still wearing a slip. 'She's still there,' I said. 'I envy her.' Lucinda said, 'She doesn't need anything but sleep.'

'Why don't you call Francis and Bertha?' I said. 'Find out what time we should pick them up on Sunday.'

'What about that Ireland thing?' she said.

'It's just a whim.'

'He seemed so serious about it.'

'I've known Francis for nine years,' I said. 'He's had

19

hundreds of enthusiasms. They're always brilliant ideas, and he is always carried away by them. And they burst within a few days, leaving anyone who changed any plans on his account a little discomfited.'

We were going to take them with us to the Island for the rest of the season. Bertha was his new girl of several months' standing, and the four of us had spent an evening together smoking dope and tripping out on travel and politics.

'Ireland's a beautiful place,' Francis had said. 'And with no history of imperialism. They're as fucked up as anybody else as people, but they've got a pretty clean national conscience.'

Lucinda got very excited. 'Yes,' she had said, 'let's get out of the country.' I knew she was thinking about the baby.

I came away from the window, and lit a cigarette. 'I don't think there's any point in going to Ireland,' I said. 'There's no peace there either. The human sickness is our addiction to fear, and we pass it on genetically. The Irish seek refuge in slavery as much as any other people. They're *Catholics*, for Christ's sake.'

'For Christ's sake?' she said.

'Not for Christ's sake. That's the problem. They've taken to religion the way the Germans took to National Socialism. But organisation is only the outer shell of fascism. And what would the four of us do there, anyway? Mope around like characters out of Lawrence? I can barely manage living with myself, and it's almost impossible with you. I'm a pervert by most standards. And you're pregnant and Bertha is into fidelity and Francis is pretending he's straight. There's just no point.'

'Why do you make things so complicated?' she asked. 'Why can't we just go to Europe like ordinary people?'

I snorted. '*Ordinary* people? I don't know any ordinary people.'

She went into the bathroom again. This time she closed the door. I poured another cup of tea. It would be several hours until I got sleepy. I didn't want to go out. I wondered how I would fill the time.

II

When, for whatever reason, a man and woman begin to live together, to share the intimacy of sex, their first contract is for exclusivity of genital contact. At first they seem to believe, and later force themselves to adhere to the notion that this human being now in constant geographical proximity has been qualitatively transformed into some property of oneself. A woman's cunt is her own, but her husband will not say so. The pristine articulated bond, arbitrary but conscious, soon succumbs to the corrosive power of habit, and the two of them are left with a smoldering possessiveness which is often tidied up into brisk, smiling hostility. The resulting years, no matter how varied in content, are riddled with the tension inherent in the psycho-emotional game known as marriage.

The most invidious myth of our civilisation is the idea that any form of social contract can substitute for unrelenting moment-to-moment awareness by each individual. Lucinda and I attempted to laugh in the face of necessity by assuming a relationship in which all the emotional glue of attachment would be dissolved by acid sophistication. But life has a way of brushing our paradigms aside.

We went back to the Island. There was immediate friction between Francis and Donna, the woman who had rented and sublet the house to us and the half-dozen other summer groupers. We dumped our bags and went into Ocean Beach, figuring that the worst way to deal with the problem would be through confrontation. We walked the narrow paths in silence, thankful to be in a place where no cars were allowed.

We went into the ice cream parlour. The vibrations were jagged and intense. I watched a teenage girl, blonde spaghettini hair, roundly fleshy hips, a soft square arse, and a look of hungry innocence in her eyes. I sat at a table with Lucinda, facing Francis and Bertha. All round us teenage America did its vapid dance. The juke box played a lament for the students shot at Kent State. 'Four dead in O-O-hio . . .' The words snaked out of a very polished rhythm section. Three pinball machines let off raucous metallic shudders. A tall, big-shouldered fifteen-year-old strode across the length of the place, wearing a jacket with 'Mobile Environment Engineer' written across the back over the Power-to-the-People fist done in bright red.

'It's amazing how in the United States every phenomenon of the left is immediately recast into a right-wing mould,' Francis said, his eyes riveted to the young Ecological Storm Trooper.

The girl I was watching looked up and our eyes flashed. Such a sweet little cunt, bulging the jeans out. And how aware of it she was, and how she said yes with such burning naïveté. My stomach dropped and I tingled clear down to my toes. Lucinda saw what was happening and feigned a look of benign amusement. I smiled insipidly at her, suddenly and fiercely hating her presence.

'It's actual theatre,' said Francis. 'I mean, it *grips* my attention.' He brought his hand up and clutched at the air, making a fist. He was a painter, but I suspected that

26

his true art lay in poetry or dance.

'It can't be painted,' he said. 'It has to be put on videotape.' He paused. 'Do you realise that painting is the last art to lose its atemporality?' I stood in salute and went to pick up the sodas.

By the time I came back, I had lost contact with the nymphet who would cry so beautifully the first time I made her realise the utter reality of the cock which lambasted the hard rubber walls of her tight shiny twat. I tried to spot her in the crowd and saw her staring into the eyes of a pre-teenage hyponist, who had sat her down and was ripping off her mind with his rap. Her face was rapt in an approximation of awe, and she was squirming in her chair.

'Ruin,' I thought. 'If I had just taken her earlier and made love to her on the beach, she would not have fallen into the hands of the Scientologists.'

The summer season was coming to a close, and the air of unreality which is the Island's major sociological feature had caught my mind. I was ready to freak out, but I felt trapped by Lucinda. Oddly, I didn't miss any particular freedom of behaviour, but was limited in the scope of my mind. As usual, this condition was accompanied by an increasing frequency of déjà vu experience, one of which surrounded me at that moment. 'I'm going back to the house,' I said.

We returned to find the other groups milling around. One family was in the small alcove off the living room. The man was a teacher of physics in high school. His total understanding of the universe seemed reduced to whatever answers appeared in the back of the textbook. His wife was a woman whose face I had no trouble forgetting after each of the hundreds of times I saw her. Their son had all the moody craftiness of the ten-year-old. And their dog, named Hot Dog, was absolutely paranoid and would bark at people for hours after they'd come into the room. They were sitting around in a fuzzy silence.

27

'Yes, that's marriage,' I thought, and felt another pang in my groin at the memory of the little girl at the ice cream parlour.

'Do you have a television set here?' Francis asked.

Lucinda and I looked at each other, and through the door into the scene in the next room. We smiled at one another.

'There it is,' she said to Francis.

The four of us sat, drinking tea and smoking grass, under a Halloween lampshade some ten feet in diameter that Donna had installed. The entire house had the air of a Hitchcock movie, although most of the dialogue was out of Beckett. Once again, it was all a play. Reality was merely real. And made up of plays within plays. Lucinda and Francis and I agreeing to a momentary perception; then Lucinda and I; then Bertha and Francis; then Francis and I. Occasionally all four of us would share the moment.

And within myself an infinity of costumes beckoned for realisation. An army of identities marching through oblivion. I became light-headed with the vision as we all sat quite still in the wooden seashell of a house, listening to the sound of waves. For a long bent instant I was held in phenomenological thrall.

In my mind I had the teenager tied to a bed: She is pure motherscreaming cunt, she is quintessence of handgripping tit, she is ultimate arse begging to be fucked. I am into a stoned De Sade head, and my cock will never get soft, not once. I go and get her and get her and get her until she is as raw as the belly of a scraped artichoke leaf. Her legs kick off into the sky. And finally she snaps the final thread and sails into the eye of the sun crying YES down the corridors of infinity while I bask in the great heat of her sacrifice and sing ME! ME! ME!

'To be divisible is to be ontological,' Francis was saying.

I looked at him. Ah yes, back to the reality of the room.

'Somehow,' I thought, 'it should be all different.' But

28

there was no context in which to plant my dissatisfaction. The conversation went on around me. 'The gun is the ultimate metaphysical argument,' I heard myself saying. I assumed that my statement somehow fitted the drift of talk we were all swaying in. 'Why aren't we fucking,' I thought, 'instead of sitting around dropping dumb words into indifferent space?'

Francis and I considered ourselves hip acidhead ex-reality trippers who had done all the scenes, and yet sexually we were as regular and as hypocritical as Methodists from southern Illinois. When I lived alone, I could be completely polymorphous perverse. But as soon as I got mated, I snapped right back into conventionally conditioned patterns, and did my swinging on the sly.

This time there was an added factor. A few weeks after Lucinda and I began living together, my doctor examined me and announced a verdict of amoebic dysentery. 'Do you have much homosexual activity?' he asked.

It wasn't a pass. He went on to declare that an epidemic was sweeping the gay world, going from arsehole to cock to mouth, or directly from arsehole to mouth, depending on circumstances and proclivities. He went through the ritual of prescription pad and somber prohibitions. 'If you want to protect yourself against this in the future,' he said, 'no more arse-licking with strangers, and don't suck any cocks unless you are sure they're clean. Wash with hot soapy water first.'

The announcement knocked me off balance. Promiscuity had been forbidden me on doctor's orders, and I was beginning what seemed to be a rational relationship with Lucinda. It seemed a good time to experiment, and I thought I would try what for me has been the greatest perversion: monogamy.

'I've decided to be faithful to you,' I said to Lucinda when I returned from his office.

'Don't do me any favours,' she said.

29

'I thought you'd be glad,' I said.

'Just fuck me enough,' she said. 'What else you do is your business.'

The edge had been shaved off my project, but I appreciated her good sense. We had known each other for six years, but vaguely, through the screen of theatre workshops which formed my most intense subterranean existence for a period during the early sixties. Several times a week I would stagger through the daisy chain of neo-Stanislavskians who flutter about the upper West Side. And on occasion I would find myself involved in some scene or exercise with Lucinda. Once, during the Theatre of Encounter's structured group gropes, I found myself sucking a big toe that I later learned belonged to her. And when we decided to spend the summer together, we were both surprised.

She stood there smiling. She had a moodily voluptuous mouth, a serious arse, and a private income. 'I think it would be very nice if you were faithful to me,' she said.

I embarked on the Yoga of Fidelity. In the beginning, the discipline was exhilarating. I felt my decision like a harness holding me in check. I chose to ignore Christ's observation that a man who lusts after a woman in his heart has already committed adultery with her, and continued to ravish most of the women I saw with my eyes. But I made no movement to act. After a while, I began to be comfortable with, and finally to enjoy, my restraint. For the first time in my life I had something which kept me from certain aspects of my sexual life.

Like a blind man who becomes sensitive to sound, I began to tune in on the more subtle vibrations of sex. Cut loose from my fixation on penetrating all orifices, I began to notice postures and textures, poses and thoughts. Women came gradually into focus as creatures whose delight far surpassed brute copulation. I started to understand moods, and the fleeting expressions of sudden

30

joy or emotional pain that would flit across a woman's face became precious to see. In stores or on the street I came to realise that hundreds of thousands of women were available all the time. Once actual fucking was barred, one could feast on all the rest that is revealed simply by how sharply or softly a woman makes a gesture, like curling her fingers to caress her lips.

But as I gained in subtlety I found myself growing in attraction for women. They might look at me quizzically, or make several attempts to approach, or begin conversations with, 'Do you mind if I speak freely?' Without willing it, I was secreting seduction. It was as though I became a woman myself. My cock having been retired from all activity except with one person, and my sexual drive sublimated into pantomime, I had no trouble being one of the girls. On a number of evenings I sat on the mattress in our bedroom on the Island, three or four women around, all of us in varying states of undress, Lucinda serving tea, the Stones playing, and the vibrations as thick as in a locker room. The softer I got, the more I lay back, the less I thought about anything at all, the more irresistible I became. I was at an exquisite edge, and the closer I hewed to my principle of fidelity the greater my options grew, and the higher the stakes of the game. The question was: when would I cash in the chips of my splintered vow?

When Lucinda announced that she was pregnant, my fantasy enlarged to almost totally overshadow reality. I would not only transmute my nature at a stroke and be monogamous, I would also enter the realm of fatherhood. The archetypal heroes trotted out to have their day. I took all the predictible trips on the mystery of heredity, and raused on the power of influence one has over a newborn infant. I ranged from the practical to the sentimental, and milked the idea of having a child for every last symbol.

Yet, at heart, I had no more feeling about it other than

an unusually sharp curiosity.

Francis was pasting collages in his diary, writing around them with multicoloured felt-tip pens. The page in front of him read, 'Suigenocide. Entropy is the final solution.' Bertha read. Lucinda was in revery.

The fantasies of faithful fatherhood had taken a long while to snap under the terrible pressures of human reality. Sexually, the hunger to be had by a man grew in my mouth and in my bowels. Lucinda couldn't fill that role. At times I would attempt to get her to sit on my face and pin my wrists down and grind her cunt into my lips and teeth. But she didn't have the energy for that, and she didn't have a cock. A few times I almost cried out to be fucked, but some force trapped the words in my throat. I needed male energy.

One afternoon, as I was sitting quietly on the sand, panic seized me. I felt trapped. No more men. No other women. Locked in the toils of a Freudian family, but now as the father instead of the child. I shrank in horror. And yet so insanely was I gripped in my own image of how I thought I would like to try being, that I couldn't break out of the prison I had built myself.

Lucinda's body began to seem like a coil of flypaper. Her skin became porous, sucking. For ten days of that period we fucked three or four times a day. Long intense dance dramas and depth contests. I was Sisyphus trying with focused anguish to get the stone balanced on top of the hill once and for all. And I reached right up to a bare millimeter of the exact top, lifting the ponderous machinery of our personalities with us. I was wrung dry of sperm and energy and desire, and she squeezed tight in an effort to suck the final drop from me. I pulled out of her cunt and crawled up so that my cock slid into her half-open mouth. She lay inert got a moment and then doubled up at the waist, covering the length of my prick in a single gulp. I sank into her throat and began to rock back and forth,

32

jerking off on her tongue. I fucked her for a very long time, in her mouth and throat and head, so deep and hard that the sperm exploded into her windpipe and she coughed and spluttered, and when she had come to, deliberately spat it out.

That night I stopped being faithful. And I began to question the widsom of letting the baby be born.

She apologised sincerely, and after that dutifully swallowed every drop of come I discharged into her mouth, but that was not the same as when we were innocent of the way in which we were meant to destroy one another. Once we had removed ourselves from the struggle to become, sex lost its urgency.

Francis and Bertha were making let's-fuck eyes at one another across the table. Lucinda announced her decision to go to bed. The people in the next room had vanished. I walked down to the beach, lay on the sand and got lost in the stars. I pulled on my cock slowly until it stirred and waited for whoever else would come down to the beach, wanting. I wondered what relationship there was between the erection in my hand and the astonishing universe expanding in searing blackness before my eyes. Reality and fantasy are never quite so right as when they are motionfully intertwined with all of their externals in one another's internals and diddling and sniggling SNORK WHEE THUD again.

III

'Krishnamurti is a moving hypnotist.'

Bosley's voice dripped in easy cadences at the other end of the line.

'But please, darling, I need you to fuck me,' I said.

'Ouugh. So free!'

He put me off and put me down in that gentle teasing way which made him so exciting. Lucinda was due back in the evening, but I was ready to swing in to the city and spend a day with Bosley. The man mood was on me again. And I wanted to yield, not to analyse. After all the years of battling with labels, I knew that any attempted judgement of sexual behaviour was stupid. And yet there was no peace. Was my desire for men an escape from my inability to make it with a woman, my fear of having a child? Or was my repeated effort at marriage a refusal to face the fact of my basic homosexuality? Instinctively, both bisexuality and celibacy seemed evasions. There was nothing for it but to continue the daily process of observation and struggle, finding out where my impulses led me.

'Why won't you let me come over?' I said.

'You're getting like a sad old whore.'

'That's all there is baby, the rest is just talk.'

'Well, then, let's talk business. What exactly do you want?'

'I want it slow and heavy, like the beat in the Mighty Quinn. You know that kind of ride?'

'Honey, this is *me* you're talking to. Umm, go ahead, I'm listening.'

'A long time for mouths, maybe a half hour. Just for kissing, for lips, for teeth, your teeth on me, and tongues, then tongues, and breath. And feeling the heat in my chest burning, making me dizzy, making me dizzy, making me weak in your arms. I rub my body against yours, squirm against you. Oh darling, please, let me hold myself against you.'

'Take your time.'

'You then, biting my nipples. You grunting in my ear. You licking the soft flesh on my inner thighs, making my knees tremble. I get small like a baby, helpless in your arms. You inserting your finger, moving it deep into me, slowly, letting me feel you, and feel that you feel me, and holding me like that, suspended, squatting, hanging, impaled on your hand, black pleasure, and your mouth on my . . . on my . . .'

'Were you going to say "cunt", baby?'

'Oh yes, my cunt.'

'That thing you got there is a cock, sweetheart. You ain't a woman. I don't like cunts.'

'Don't push me away.'

'Suck it.'

'Yes, make me go down on you. Such a long time on your cock. Sliding my tongue in the hollow of your throat and licking your hard chest, tasting the salty sweat on your belly, lapping over all your skin, into the musk of your hair, and finally having your beautiful cock in my mouth. For such a long time. Slippery warm thing. Mother's nipple.

38

Father's censored place. The soft of the ridged rim. The bulk of it in my throat, gagging, suck, oh my Cock, oh my most Eternal Cock. Whimpering, Shuddering. And strength from your burning onto my lips. Let . . . me . . . lick . . . it. . . . Fuck me in the mouth, stuff your cock in my mouth, put your arse on my mouth, hit my mouth . . .'

'Baby, you off inside your head again.'

'Then bring me out, make me real. Take control of me, use me, hold me. Slide down so our bodies feel the length of each other. Put your hardness between my thighs. Feel me open. Feel my legs part and raise up for you. Put it at the opening. Fuck me. Fuck me in the arse. Do it now.'

'Oohhhh, Jeeeessssussss.'

'It's all yours. I raise my arse so your cock can more beautifully sink hotly in. Your eyes burn into mine. I can't hold myself any longer. I am slipping and slipping. Oh, excuse me, let this wave of rapture pass.'

'That's once. You going to come a hundred times tonight before I'm finished.'

'Stupid prick, it's not you who does it, it's me. I let you make me come.'

'Get on your belly, bitch.'

'Yes, now I can't defend, I can't hold back. Your knees come in against the backs of my knees. How you strain into me, how your cock excites me. You slant it up, and then thrash to each side, and then slant it down. You cover all the inside of my hole. You fuck me thoroughly. Jolts of electric fire run through me. My fingers twitch and I bite the pillow. I am being fucked. I am being fucked. There is nothing in the world but being fucked. Now you call me. You have me look into your eyes. I look back over my shoulder, my neck bent like a bird's, and your wet warm mouth covers mine. My legs open more, and I feel you between them; you push your pelvis between my cheeks; I feel your hip bones against my arse, your cock inside me, inside me. I am naked to you. Open and bent,

39

my cunt completely empty to your thrust. My cunt. My breasts are punishers for your hands, my mouth a receptacle for your spit, my eyes the record of my thought. You know it all. I am you. I have incorporated you. You push me to my knees. You hit hard at the deep tender spot. I feel pain. I hurt. I beg you continue. I push into you. Oh, snarling black animal at my neck. Oh, fuck me now. I give you now. Fuck me now. I have me now. And all the sounds I make into the night as you gyrate and erupt inside me.'

There was a long slience.

Then a low laugh.

'Baby, you are *too much*.' He paused. 'But I just can't make it today. When are you coming to the city next?'

'Maybe ten days.'

'Call me,' he said. And we hung up.

The problem is confusion. What is one to do with a club foot of salad? All my attempts to deal with living as a problem embroiled in technology, either of metal or of the mind. And I couldn't find the relationship between seriousness and silliness. The leaders laugh, but they have no humour.

I sometimes want and sometimes do not want. When I want, I move towards the process of consumption, romantically known as sharing. I seek out those people who have complementary need, and we service one another's vacuums. This is simple commerce. All the rest of it is soap opera for the slaves. Obvious truth, distorted by the masters, comes to seem contemptible in the face of sanctimonious official lies.

What was I to make of my shamelessly flinging myself at Bosley? What relation did that have in relation with my relation with Lucinda? With her, in the beginning, the pattern was classic: giving-and-giving, giving-and-taking, taking-and-giving, taking-and-taking, and mutual isolation. Every exchange we had, from fucking to fighting, fit this paradigm. The honeymoon period released in us enough energy for me to see the structures clearly. But she got sloppy, and I got lazy, and our days lost their sharpness.

It was becoming clear that I was interested in the dynamics of interaction with people, and the accompanying changes within myself, and it made almost no difference who the other person was, so long as he or she maintained a certain level of energy for the period we were together. In short, the person was not important, merely the person's effects.

When Lucinda and I began fucking, there was always fireworks. The first penetration past the tightness, the joy of discovery, the plunge into virgin virginity. Then there was the race through the Kama Sutra, working out all the possible acrobatics. 'Look, you get into a full Plow posture, and I'll support myself on the windowsill, and enter you from above and behind, and oh?! oh! OH!!' and etc. And when we had finished with all that we were left with the boredom which attaches to the stick when all the ice cream has been licked off. Then, no matter what rationalisations came to the fore, it was simply time to get it on with someone else, fresh energy, new variations. I had come a long way away from simple values.

My consciousness seemed to have become the product of the story. To me, life was a book, was a film. I lived in the physical centres and the mind. The only emotion I didn't find vulgar was cosmic sadness, ultimate poignancy. And I have had the full spectrum of advice, from the intimate friends to therapists to gurus, and they said things like, 'You're schizoid,' or 'You've lost touch with the Other,' or 'You're afraid of your feelings.' Yet, what of it? Can I be other than I am? Not all birth defects are physical. To be crippled in the emotions is as real as to be crippled in the limbs. One does not say to a man with a paralysed leg, 'Why don't you run?' Then why does one ask of a man with a heart hardened through too much sensitivity shattered, 'Why do you weep?'

Francis came downstairs.

'And you're even colder than I am,' I said.

'Bertha's sleeping late. What shall we do?' he said.

We set out to walk to Cherry Grove together, three miles down the long strand of white sand and stunning blue sky with clouds, and the constant swish of wind and tumbling waves. The Grove was the cultural centre of the Island where the homosexuals had claimed a township of their own.

'Can you imagine what it would be like if all the homosexuals were given a state, say, Wyoming, and could set up whatever kind of society they wanted?' I said.

Francis smiled to himself, setting up the projector in his own mind. 'The first overwhelming mood would be one of exhilaration,' he began.

'Right, the seeming freedom from all sexual restraints, the new sense of purpose, the rapture of discovering a sanctioned identity.'

He nodded. 'It would probably come together under some charismatic leader, a gay Lenin. MetaFag. The queer Moses.'

We came to the first house which marks the beginning of the Grove after the long stretch of government preserve known as the Sunken Forest. The vibrations changed drastically, instantly. The people lying on the blankets in this area were not pretending, as did the denizens of the straight sections of the beach, that nothing was happening except what could pass muster on the family TV show. Here, the sense of presence was palpable. Everyone was aware of being there, and how he was there, and how he saw others being there, and how they received him. A constant flutter of extremely subtle communications in the most sophisticated body language went on all the time. The air was charged with attentiveness. My skin bristled. I looked over at Francis.

His face was set in a mask of unperception, as though this were merely a place to look at, not to relate to. I wondered whether he was actually straight. His drawings denied it, as did occasional oblique comments. I assessed him physically, and found to my surprise, no intimation of sex. I couldn't penetrate my own condition to sufficient depth to know to what degree I was suppressing desire. Given our extraordinary closeness, fucking ought to have been the natural conclusion, yet we hardly ever even touched. Perhaps it was a tacit understanding on both our parts that the absolute lack of sexual involvement is what allowed our friendship to continue.

'The entire sociology would be arranged differently,' he continued. 'There would be almost no provision necessary for children, and the nature of education would change radically. Time would tend to disappear.'

'I wonder whether the sexes would be integrated?'

'There would be no overt or legal discrimination, but a subtle sexual apartheid would insinuate itself, and male and female ghettoes would come into being.'

I grew excited. 'Imagine the scenes when the new nation begins. The wild and open cruising, the public lovemaking. Total euphoria.'

Francis drew in a sharp breath and seemed to snap to. For the first time he registered his surroundings. 'So this is Cherry Grove,' he said.

'You sound disappointed,' I said.

He looked over at me. The obvious had suddenly become seductive. There was nothing to stop us now from stepping into the act itself. Then there would be no barriers. And perhaps the problems with the women would dissolve. Yet, as we hovered at the edge, a blinding sense of impossibility paralysed our wills, and we said no to the new, refusing to transform it into the old.

'It's better not even to bother,' he said. 'I need one person at least that I don't have to pretend sexual passion

43

to.' He paused. 'And anyway, you're not my type.'

We cut in from the beach and walked down the boardwalk in silence for a few minutes. 'And then,' Francis began again, 'they discover that they still need people to take away the garbage, and that they have to put together some form of monetary system, and they have to get into the whole supply and demand hassle with food, and that they have hostile neighbours.' He paused. 'The rest is history. The bright ones learn how to get the stupid ones to do all the shitty jobs. They gather power and hypnotise the rest with the rituals of government and religion. And they find that they are addicted to hatred and violence and lust and guilt and jealousy and all the sins which are part of the human heritage. There is dissatisfaction. Radical groups challenge the established authority. Heresies arise. And a new voice is heard calling for the rights of bisexuals to be respected. But MetaFag dies and the faggot Stalin comes into power. Executions happen. Happy Homoland becomes another tyranny.'

I laughed. 'Imagine how things would have been if people like Trotsky were gay and . . .'

Francis turned and pinned me with one of his steely looks. 'Oh, Trotsky was gay,' he said. I was caught up short. It seemed stupid to wonder whether he was putting me on. I took him for a tour of the bars and scenic sights, and for a walk through the meat rack. But he got very uptight, and we left quickly, to trudge three miles back to Seaview.

When we got back to the house, Lucinda had returned and was in a panic. But it was general, and she had no way of letting herself know how she felt. I was too taken by the scope of the day to notice where she was at. She latched on to me and made herself unpleasant in unspecified ways. It was as though she were a child and just wanted to be picked up and held. But at the time I didn't see that. That's the whole of the matter. I just didn't

44

see what she needed. And she was unable to ask.

We began bickering, and then arguing. I went into the bedroom. She followed, and within seconds we were shouting at one another. I began to walk out. She grabbed my arm. 'Let me go,' I yelled. 'Don't you see my state? If I don't get out of here, I'm going to hurt you.'

A revelation crossed her face.

'You want to be hurt, don't you?' I said. 'Well no,' I shouted, 'I'm not going to play that game, I'm not going to beat you up.'

I turned to go and again she grabbed my arm. I went blind with rage. I flung her from me. She threw herself at my legs. I yanked her head up by the hair, lifted her bodily, and threw her back on the bed. She fell on her spine and lay there for a moment in total open confusion. I felt a charge of sexual energy. I leapt on her and slapped her very hard across the face, two times, three times. And then I jumped back and ran from the room.

I stayed away for over an hour, and when I returned she was wiggly and warm, wanting to cuddle. I was, in turn, properly gruff and tender.

It is appalling the way in which we mechanically trip through the most tawdry scenarios. And still there is no escape. Knowing what we do seems to have no effect on our continuing to do it. What if I killed her one day in just the same manner I had beat her up? Such things happen. The single most apparent item in the jumble of our interaction is the fact the ante is continually being raised. There are more convincing ways of travelling through the void than on a see-saw.

Perhaps we would be fucking. She would be straining to have every conceivable portion of me imbedded in her. I would be struggling with the desire to immolate her and the opposing fear of having her drag me into her own pit. I could see how it would start. . . .

I push her face down into the pillow, squashing her

45

mouth out of shape, while she laps at the palm of my hand and sucks my fingers. My hand forms a fist and I push down harder. I begin to hurt her. She digs her nails into my back, simultaneously returning the pain and edging me on to greater devastations of herself. I punish her cunt with my cock. I don't move my pelvis. I institute a constant insistent push, letting her squirm to impale herself more deeply. The rivers of black flame cascading in mountainous wild waves from the sexual fusion destroy the stage and theatre where our images work out their drama, and violence bursts the bonds of fantasy. I rear back and smash my knuckles into her mouth. A tooth breaks, a lip is torn.

Within a few months I am beating her regularly and pissing in her mouth every day and forcing her to eat her food on her hands and knees from the floor. I bring men to the house and force her into acts of mediocre pornography with them. Her addiction for the depraved grows. And one day, mostly out of ennui, I kill her.

Lucinda made dinner and the four of us sat down to eat. Francis began to tell some of the adventures of the day's trip, including our discovery of a bird sleeping in the middle of one of the walks. 'It was just sitting there,' he said, 'with its beak under its wing, sleeping, I mean, right in the middle of the path. And I bent down and said, "Can we help you?", and it took its beak out from under its wing, shook its head, looked at us, and flew away. I found it extraordinary. Absolutely extraordinary.' And he said the final word with heartwarming relish.

Bertha looked at him. 'What kind of bird was it?'

A look of perplexity crossed his face, giving him a glazed expression. 'I don't think that's a relevant aspect of the story,' I said.

'Oh,' she exclaimed, 'but I want to *picture* the bird. And Francis describes things so well. What did the bird look like, Francis?' she keened.

46

He shook his head. The blade was in his belly. 'Uh, it was kind of a small brown bird,' he said, and looked to me for support. But I was not in the mood to help him humour Bertha's hurt. Especially when she expressed her pain as hostility. Lucinda and I went into the bedroom to fuck.

We got undressed rapidly and I lay down on my back. She got on top and lowered her cunt onto my erection. She was very wet and hot. The wild mood changes of the day had turned her on. She swallowed my cock whole, and began to rock her pelvis back and forth, using my pubic bone as a fulcrum. She moved back and up, and then forward and down so that I felt like she was sucking at me with her cunt. I slapped her arse, lightly at first, and then harder, between the cheeks and over her arsehole and cunt. At one point I hit my balls with the tip of my finger and felt a crazy jagged pain shoot through me. I felt an anger that was not directed at any particular person, and I shouted out again and again as she continued to fuck me. Her face was calm, impassive. Her breasts were gloating and bouncing off her chest like water balloons, and only the contractions in her belly showed that she came again and again and again, before I turned my face to one side and let myself shoot off into her.

I felt, immediately afterwards, as I used to feel as a child when I had finished masturbating and believed that I had committed a mortal sin. Even fucking had become corrupted. The timbre of the time had changed. I realised that I was becoming hard, and even when I thought of social change, my mind went immediately to dynamite. But I was frightened by my own violence, and by the violence which would be unleashed in the society if I were so to act. Time, chronological time, moves through me no matter what I do. I am a thing of duration. Within my allotted space, the options are open. Do I wish to commit murder? Do I wish to man the barricades? The opportunity for any form of intensity of theatre I desire is available. And survival comes only through a miracle.

We got dressed and went back into the living room. We didn't look into one another's eyes at all. Donna was there, dressed in black leather pants and suede shirt, with a thick red leather belt and long violet cape. She was six feet tall.

'Anybody want to go bicycle riding with me?' she said.

Francis shot her a surreptitious glance and then looked over at Bertha, whose frozen smile could not mask the gleam of animal cunning in her eyes as she studied the outrageously electric woman who stood in the middle of the floor, lacking only a whip to complete her role. His defeat was small but exquisite. He looked down into his lap and pretended he hadn't even heard the question.

'I'll go,' Lucinda said.

She needed to let the open air absorb some of the energy flooding her. The fuck had satisfied one hunger, but aroused another. I wished she could get Donna to bed and let me participate, or at least watch. Another body in bed would not solve any problems, but would certainly contain them for pleasant periods of time. I was ready for escape, even the obvious, the trite.

The two women left, and Francis leaned back in his chair, his eyes closed. Bertha looked around for someone to hate. 'We're robots,' I said, 'Press the buttons and we react. We've all been programmed for opacity from birth.'

I went out to the porch and smoked one cigarette after another. Despite all the literature and propaganda, despite my own training to the contrary, sex was not for me a matter of personality. When I'm looking down at a moaning, churning arse, and I am loving each moment of strange glorious contact with the human being who sports that arse, and I am cock-happy with the wonder of our dance, I really don't care what the other person's name is. I don't even care what my own name is. Ecstasy has no name.

'You woman, whoever you are, the idiosyncrasies of your life story are something I will be pleased to share when our heads are on the pillow. For the moment of time I share geographic space with you, I will respect your uniqueness, and be alert to not making life any more difficult for you or me than it need be. But when we fuck, you are all women to me. You are every black and yellow and red and white and tall and short and thin and fat and old and young and frightened and fearsome and mother and daughter and rapture and terror that is you, woman. And if in the midst of our transport, one of your bodies is moved away and another put in its place, do you think I am going to stop to notice the difference, except in the ways I must change to relate to the new you most fully?

'And you, man do you imagine when I am down, I mean way down, I mean all the way down, on your cock, it matters to whom that cock is attached, except in the degree of sensitivity that you show in relation to our intimate communion and communication?

'A tongue is a tongue is a tongue is a tongue. The language it speaks when it does not serve as a handmaid to the word is what translates my soul. The problem of relationship ceases to be a problem when personality becomes the crucible in which being refines its awareness. Sex reaches its fullest expression when it strikes like lightning to suffuse the space with silence.'

I thought, and got up to make myself a cup of coffee, and drank it very slowly while I smoked three more Gauloises. 'It's time to give up smoking soon,' I said to myself.

Francis and Bertha walked past me, self-consciously aware that I knew that they had healed the rift and were going upstairs to fuck. 'How tedious we all are,' I thought.

'I wonder how I feel right now?' I said out loud.

I felt like a dirty dishrag thrown into the greasepit under a sink. 'I've felt better,' I thought, 'and I've felt worse.'

49

I imagined that things, then, were pretty good, or not too bad. There was no way to know for sure.

IV

Perhaps we have entered a period of annihilation politics. The only true revolutionary is the one who affects a life style which takes the imminent destruction of the entire species as a basic premise. We who have awakened from the mist of anomalous obscurity which hypnotises the mass of manwomankind form the true danger to those who require the maintenance of social systems to sustain their power. But the rulers are safe, for the people are conditioned to follow, and only the brutal presume to rule.

By all my principles, the foetus which now grew in Lucinda's womb had a complete right to life. I held no grudge against the thing, and in a general way, I wished it well. But if its birth were to serve to crystallize Lucinda's emotional dependence on me, then it could not be allowed to join us. And she did not want to be tied to the process of raising a child without my support and help.

'Night after night in that apartment with a baby! I'm already isolated to the point of going crazy. That would kill me,' she said.

For my part, I wanted no long term marriage with her. That hadn't been my intention when we moved in together.

The child was a mockery of our purpose. But its existence raised a serious question. If it were my life against its, I would not have hesitated for a second to dispatch it. But it was my *life style* against its *life*. Was *how* I lived more important than *that* it lived? Did it point to some essential defect within my person that I could not allow this infant to come into the world and maintain myself as well?

All my Catholic conditioning rose up to join a febrile imagination to see the foetus in its human development. I could not think about it without picturing it, in anatomic detail, in spiritual context.

There were never these problems in the Japanese whorehouses. Walking into a room with twenty or thirty women, young and soft, with such sweet stoppered eyes made of almonds. Music and sequined gowns, the smells of perfume and incense, and everywhere the glowing flesh, the golden flesh moving thigh against thigh, breast against bra cup, buttock against buttock. The mouths that watched and the hands that told.

The simple availability of the women was breathtaking. An introduction, fifteen or twenty minutes of pleasant conversation, and a brief exchange of money, made the prelude to a long evening of bathing and tea and sweetcakes, many hours of delicious oriental fucking, exquisite and internal. The tender wrinklings of their nipples and the cupped shudders of their cunts would ride you for hours into the most delicate bliss.

The choice of the evening could be a specialist in oral sex, and would suck and nibble your cock for what seemed an eternity or two. She seemed to have an instinct for the closeness of ejaculation, and could bring you to tears by licking the tip of your cock until you were sure you would come, had to come – and then she would let it go. The sperm subsided still bubbling down the centre of your cock, and you tingled in absolute pleasure for five or ten minutes. And then she would begin again, different, more. And

54

when you came, it did subsume all the near orgasms before it. It actually was like a flow of molten lava exploding from your cock. And she drank it in wildly, joyfully. It was what she had been preparing for so long, like a master cook delicately testing the fragility of a pie crust as it bakes. And you realised that she liked doing this, she thrived on it. And you wondered how you would ever again be able to come inside a woman who was less than utterly enthusiastic.

Or you might take home a yellow version of the girl next door, and when you took her to bed find out that she was a crazy who wanted to lick the shit off your arsehole, and bit you so hard on the chest that the skin broke and blood flowed, and you hit her four or five times to make her puff off into some private ecstasy and let you do whatever you wanted with her body. And you played out every picture of degradation you had ever fantasised.

Or you might fall in love.

'Yoshie?'

The thin girl turned lazily in her half-sleep, her eyes still closed, the dim light making her skin seem like stone, her face relaxed like that of a great bronze Buddha.

'Hai. Nani?' she said.

'I want you.'

'Oh.'

It came out as a moaned whisper. You touched her. There was a long still moment, and she was suddenly upon you, as quickly as the movement of a striking snake. Always like that with her. She was always ready, always attentive. She cared for you the way a tree produces fruit, without thought, without consideration.

And so you married her, and when you got back to the United States, suddenly everything was ugly again. You were ugly, she was ugly, life was a constant intimidation, and in confused frustration you walked out one afternoon, and she spent nine years recovering before she could let another man into her heart, and you still wonder whether you will ever know another woman like that. Was she the fabled only-one that is supposedly allotted to each of us?

Captivated by the convolutions of the contest, I forgot to notice the nature of the arena. With deadening regularity I mistook the drama for the dharma. As Francis put it, 'Everyone's begun to confuse the collective subjective with the objective.'

The next afternoon was timeless. The sun spoke geometrically from the sky and the earth felt cosy. There was no hint of the endless blackness of space or the vastnesses through which our planet plummets in its chaotic whirlings. I sat alone in the living room, watching the light contour the space into segments. The forty-year-old Seaview houses stood like hunchbacked rocks. And from one long wall of windows, I could see the dunes which led to the water.

Lucinda had gone to visit her two daughters again who were just returning from camp. Her marriage had been prototypic. She was the debutante daughter of a wealthy lawyer and his dog-show addict of a wife. Her husband was the very successful, very bored, Long Island Jewish doctor. She played the scene for fourteen years, with the proper costumes, the proper lines, and the proper number of lovers. And one morning woke up to find that she was suffocating and had been dying of dryness for a long time.

After a reflex consideration of what she supposed was her duty, she realised that she had absolutely no feeling at all for her husband, and only a detached interest in the future development of her children. 'I knew that if they stayed with him they would at least get the best in food, clothing, and shelter, go to good schools and all that shit. And I had nothing to offer them but inarticulate disillusionment.' Such was her reasoning.

She left that day. And when all the shock had subsided and the legalities were arranged, she opted for a cash settlement and left him with a house, the cars, the daughters, the social matrix of his days, and a new girlfriend whom he soon married. She spent a year doing nothing, becoming promiscuous with men who would call her at three in the morning because they felt like fucking and knew she was available. Then she met me. And got pregnant again. ('The diaphragm must have slipped' – laughter.)

During the first few weeks when we were telling one another enough of our life stories to provide at least an outline, I met her parents. They had long ago reached that state, so common, where marriage is a wearying, but necessary, truce. Her father had relinquished all power in the pleasantly baroque West Side suite they lived in, and in the Berkshire estate, and in the matter of such choices as to which countries to visit on this year's European trip. He devoted himself to the intricacies of corporate law and the vagaries of the stock market, and counted himself blessed on those days when his lower back didn't pain him too much.

I got invited to the country place one weekend, and spent a dada evening with Lucinda, her mother, a gay psychiatrist, and his neurotic dog. The most interesting thing was that I didn't perceive that the doctor was a fag. He was the most perfectly disguised closet queen I had ever seen, and I admired his total camouflage. At one point we went into the woodshed for kindling, and as we stumbled around in the dark, we both began tingling. I felt it and knew he felt it. He reached out and put his hand on my arse. But he had been drinking a lot and it turned me off.

In front of the fire he told psychiatrist stories, and was very amusing. He had the wit of a man who has found a place, no matter how uncomfortable, to stand.

'She's been with me for ten years,' he said, talking of a patient.

'Isn't she cured yet?' Lucinda asked.

57

'No,' he said, and laughed. 'She's still under the delusion that I can help her.'

'Do you have any homosexual patients?' I asked.

And Lucinda's mother laced me with a glance of rankling hatred. But he held my gaze. 'I don't consider homosexuality a neurosis,' he said.

'Merely an inconvenience?'

The secret life is the substantial life: the things we do, the feelings coursing through us, which we share with no one. It is most clearly felt in the moments just after awakening in the morning, when we press our fingertips to our lips and hold ourself with figure-ground fragility. We know it best as loops of terror swing through our minds just before sleep. It is most agonising and glorious when we are among others, and we sit in perfect self-possession, sensing the weight of the body in the chair, aware of the many levels of perception and the echelons of being, watching the others in their unconscious sniffings and meanderings around one another's sleepwalking toes. The secret life is what the policeman would arrest us for, and the priest punish us for, and the lover pursue us for. We have become addicted to the outside and the hard; the inside and the soft have become rare and precious moods. And fetch a high price among the savage and jaded experience junkies of our age.

When I go into the Baths, I often enter the universe of the private. My centre of gravity descends to my belly, my walk becomes slow, my glance is minimally seductive. I would be stamped shallow by the public worlds, the world of politics, the world of society, the world of power, the world of identity.

The joy of fucking lies only secondarily in ejaculation orgasm. Rather it is in the beauty of the woman's face when it melts and becomes unfamiliar, when she ceases to have a feature, and becomes the embodiment of mystery, the edge of knowing. In that space, she shows her single purest gesture, the actual curve of her soul, and one can see her in the totality of her shining complex self, radiant in admission of all that she is.

Essential human intelligence lies for me in the gleam of awareness in the eyes of one who is at the point of surrendering to a flow of passion. It has nothing to do with the patriarchal insanity over achievement. It is the slightest of pressures, the most delicate of textures.

All day long a single peace pervaded the house. Francis and Bertha were resting on the sand; Donna was off on one of her baroque cruises, tracking down the most blatant oddities of the Island's social fare. Thoughts swept in and out of my mind like the waves whose voice never ceased, not even for a second. Released from the need to use thought for any technological activity, I saw the substance of thought as light and airy. Great shimmering castles of fantasy proliferated before my inner eye. I was, then, master of all thought forms. Architecture flowed freely. Entire universes of discourse were caught and understood and dispensed in microseconds of chronological time. The computer sang.

I stepped into the land of the ideal, without for a moment losing the reality of the physical world of which I knew myself to be but a brief manifestation, me and all my fancy thoughts. The elusive face of ultimate reality smiled at me from behind the veils of the last few words still sawing wood in my brain. And then, at a stroke, I was cut loose. Past all conceptual boundaries, past all modes and moods, and into the embrace of pure being.

Francis and Bertha walked in. 'Hey man, you look stoned,' he said.

'You know, whenever I think I've got it, that's when I don't.'

'It's a long way to Tipperary,' he said.

I went down to the beach. It occurred to me that the thing which made Francis so valuable a friend was that he knew that any given state *is* that state, and only a fool wonders which label to apply to it. Enlightened or stoned? You can tell by the degree to which the person is trying to figure it out.

As I stepped onto the sand, paranoia closed over me like a giant clam shell. The people on the shore were all alien. Something was wrong with them, unspeakably wrong. I could find no rationalisation. To my horror, someone smiled at me. I smiled back. And then I was giggling uncontrollably. The hilarity of it was overwhelming. 'They'll think I'm crazy,' I thought.

I went back to the house. Some people had arrived, and as I walked in the door they began speaking to me, making noises with their mouths, hitting me with their words. With a great tearing of gears I shifted levels and entered the world of question and answer. I found myself holding my mind in a knot, wishing over and over again that Lucinda would return early.

V

She came in on the eight o'clock ferry. We embraced and held on to one another for a long while. Our needs this time were in absolute synchrony.

The house was in pandemonium. All of the groupers had arrived for the weekend, and with guests, some thirteen people plus dogs were milling around the living room and kitchen. Everyone was smiling and polite, but the level of irritation was high. Donna was at the phone in the corner of the room, watching the crowd with calculating eyes.

'That bastard is having a party tonight,' she shouted at me as Lucinda and I walked in.

'Who?' I said, exaggerating the word with my lips so she could see what I was saying from across the noisy room.

'That millionaire bastard on the corner. And the fucker hasn't invited me.' She spoke into the phone and hung up. 'I was over there this afternoon,' she said, walking towards us. Her voice dropped to a whisper. 'In that scummy swimming pool of his. And I was coming up the ladder when he swam past and grabbed my arse. I turned around. "I sure would like to eat you," he said. So I told him to open his mouth, I had to take a shit anyway.'

'Yeah, well, I wouldn't invite you to the party either.'

'The summer's not over yet,' she said. 'I'll fix him.'

Donna was one of the few consciously realised paranoids I had ever met. Her entire approach towards other people was based on a meter which registered somewhere around her solar plexus. It had three indications on it: friend, neutral, and enemy. 'You have to trust your instinct,' she said at least five times a day. 'You know when you can't trust someone. You can tell it in the first flash. Always go by that. Get him before he gets you.'

'Do you want to eat?' Lucinda asked.

'Why don't you throw in with us?' This from Donna who had no trouble with any change of subject. 'It'll be in about an hour. We have shrimp.'

'Then let's go fuck first,' I said to Lucinda.

She smiled. Her eyes were clear and warm. The purple bruise on the spot where I had hit her had faded, and she looked like a cover for a Billie Holiday album.

'You have a good time with the kids?' I asked.

'It was all right. They said that if I had a boy friend they wouldn't want to talk to him.'

'Terrific,' I said.

'I went to visit an old friend, and talked to her about us. She's forty-five and very wise. She said that you'll have to kill me. That either I'll get out of your space or you'll kill me.'

'Go join Women's Lib,' I said. 'Not the bra corps agitating for higher pay. But the ones who are trying to find out what psychological dependence is all about. Get free.'

But, as almost always, my words were the prelude to a seduction. And soon we were on the bed, kissing and holding. Our clothes got shrugged and tugged off. And for a while we fucked very tenderly, remembering each other, being gentle with one another. Then it was as though some trigger were pulled. Her legs shot up and I plunged deep

64

into her cunt, and we were grunting and groaning like drunken wrestlers. She wrapped her calves around my thighs and rode hard and fast until she came. Her orgasm had the abrupt quality of the way in which a man will flick a cigarette butt into the street. I waited until her vibrations fell off, and then continued my movement inside her until I reached a climax.

'We've never come together,' she said.

'Well, we're living in a fascist country. What can you expect?'

We lay quiet for a while, enjoying the silence which stretched for great distances around the room. 'I got arrested earlier tonight,' I said. 'For riding a bicycle in Ocean Beach. It cost me fifteen dollars to bail out the bike and I have to go for a hearing tomorrow. It was the old cop. The sergeant. He came scooting down the path on his three-wheel scooter and nabbed me just as I crossed the line into Seaview. It was ridiculous. You should have seen him, old enough to be a grandfather, dressed in that silly blue suit, chasing people on bicycles.'

'Where were you going?'

'I was coming back from buying some grass. So he escorted me all the way back to the station, and I waited right next to the fucking jail for an hour while some automaton got ready to make out a ticket, and all the while I've got two ounces in my pocket.'

I lit a cigarette. I was now feeling the anger I had laughed off earlier in the day. 'I really wanted to kick his teeth in.'

'But he had a gun,' Lucinda said.

'Right. He had a gun.' I let the scene come together in my mind. 'And when I came out of that cracker box they use for a station, a lady came up to me and started laying a rap on my head. "Isn't it a shame?" she kept saying. And another guy came up and before I knew it we had a political rally going, denouncing the police and the courts, fists waving in the air. A pack of frightened middle-class wage slaves and one crazy on Fire Island shouting against rule by authority. It was incredibly trivial and glorious all at once. And people think they'll recognise fascism when the cops start talking German. It's here. America is a reform school.'

'What are you going to do at the trial?' she asked.

'Make a speech questioning the foundation of American law and the premises of western civilisation.'

Lucinda yawned. 'Let's see if Donna has dinner ready,' she said.

She went towards the closet to get a dress. 'You'll see,' I said. 'One day you'll wake up and discover that you haven't had an original thought, or an unconditional emotion, or a spontaneous action for a long time. You will have become a robot, a walking typewriter ribbon for government and industry and the military to use in any fucking way they want. And they will smile as they dig our graves. And the worst part is that they won't be any more intelligent than the billions of people they control; merely more crucial.

'Do you think we're having such a hard time just because we're maladjusted individuals? The whole culture is sick at its core. So distorted that there is no way to even remember what a healthy human being is like. No wonder our fucking is so mechanical. The ultimate American sexual scene will come when jailors give acid to chicks in prisons and watch them go down in a final burst of masochistic self-degradation to suck their cocks, while they hold a pistol barrel to their temples and watch the tears of relief spring from their eyes.'

Lucinda turned and there were tears in her eyes. 'And what about the baby?' she said.

I rocked with the emotion that hurtled between us. I hung my head. 'That's the real question, isn't it? Not whether we get our rocks off together.'

It was to be a boy. We had both flashed on that

66

simultaneously one night. And we were going to call him Dante G. He could fill in the middle initial with any number of names he wanted at different times in his life, a mobile nomenclature. I desired to see him born, yet would take no responsibility for his upbringing. He would need food and shelter and fondling; he would need a certain stability to keep from being swept away by the winds of thought and circumstance. But I could barely manage such essentials for myself, and Lucinda resented the impositions introduced by a helpless infant. She most certainly did not want to be burdened with its care if I were not going to be around to help. We did not have a means in our culture by which a child could grow up without being a drag much of the time, and so it might be better to spare everyone concerned the hassle of dealing with an odious situation.

Except that such reasoning shrivelled before the fact of the foetus who by then had both overall shape and fingernails.

There is the classic scene in which the fond parents are lying in bed reading. Suddenly, the wife turns to the husband and says, 'It's kicking, here feel it,' and she places her hand on her belly. But to have felt that child moving in Lucinda's stomach would have driven me mad.

I wondered whether I would ever break through the walls of ego involvement without losing my individuality? And why did I hold this individuality in such high esteem anyway? It became an academic question when I realised that I had no power to shape my life in any meaningful sense. I could only remain alert and attempt to stay out of the way of my natural unfolding. And if that happened to be in the direction of fey expectations, what was I to do? I found myself taking refuge in habit, or decadence. The sexual act itself was becoming a chore from which I could not free myself. I had begun to lose my passion, and was beginning to stoke the fires of hatred in myself in order to feel something strongly enough to have a sense of being alive. But hate leads to fear, which merges into self-pity. And to expiate, once again I would use my cock as a club to punish Lucinda's cunt for daring to introduce new life into the world, and she would allow herself to sink deep into guilt.

The only advantage homosexual sex seemed to have over all this was that it took place between people who had a more precious understanding of one another's desperation. I have punished women, and meant it; I have punished men, but never forgotten it was theatre. For me, the man who slaps my face is helping me to get my scene together; the woman who rakes my back wants literally to destroy me.

Desire turns appreciation into exploitation, which destroys the sensitivity of perception. And desire lives in a cave, and rarely sees the stars.

When Lucinda and I began living together, she closed off all the other avenues of her life. She stopped doing her photography ('I dig you so much that I don't even want to look at my cameras anymore.') and gave up all her lovers ('You're all I need baby.') and in general acted as though all the problems of her life had neatly been solved by my arrival. I understood that she was, as we all are, the victims of historical conditioning, but that didn't make her any easier to live with. In order to have my own freedom, it was imperative that she have hers, even to the point of fucking other men. I was willing to accept the pain of jealousy in order to escape the grey suffocation of exclusivity.

But I was not as strong as my word either. For every time she lapped my cock with her half-open mouth or subtly invited me to fuck her in the arse, I betrayed my position for another go-round on the sensation carousel. When I fucked her, I gave her everything I could muster at the moment, and in my head was the single vibration of possession: '*This is mine.*' I stayed with her through all her changes; I took everything, inhaling her through my pores. I installed myself with my cock and fingers and tongue. I blew her mind and blasted her body and she became so absorbed in the process that she forgot who she was.

I knew what was happening and I played the game. For what man doesn't like to have a woman melt into him after orgasm and say, 'There has never been a man like you?' I accepted her adulation each time I fucked her well, and then would complain because my intensity robbed her of her centre.

With me, after the initial period of infatuation, a good fuck with the woman I'm living with becomes just that. It's no different, in its way, from a fine meal or a stunning sunset. But with her, whoever she happens to be, fucking gets all entangled with emotions. And, of course, the practical result of fucking: children.

'I don't know,' I said to Lucinda. 'It's as much your baby as it is mine. Why do you keep looking at me for a final decision on the matter? What do you want to do?'

'I won't know until the last minute,' she said.

'The last minute!' I shouted. 'It's already past three months now. In a while they won't even do an abortion. You'll have the baby by default.'

She looked very sad.

'There's a way,' she said. 'It's a thing they do with fluid. They can abort you even into the fifth month.'

She looked at me, waiting for me to say the words which would redeem the child, but I shivered inside myself.

'I'll make reservations at the hospital,' she said.

She dressed and left the bedroom. I lit another cigarette and sat on the window ledge. The thoughts came succinctly, a collage of the day's events.

'Am I a criminal if I refuse to assume the role which is necessary to give Lucinda the support she needs to have the baby? Not in any judicial sense, but existentially. If I knowingly commit the act, or omit the act, which leads to having the baby flushed out of the womb, I have ended the life of another human being.'

And then, 'And if I follow that path, doesn't a new door open for me in the corridors of action? For if I kill my own child, why should I hesitate at obliterating any of the monsters who strangle freedom in the name of authority?'

I thought of the arrest, and the next morning's trial, and the condition of the species, and of Lucinda's pain, and of Dante's poor chances of survival, and murder formed in my heart.

'I have burst quietly past almost every boundary,' I thought. I was at a point where I could find no reference point for value, and was fast slipping into the stream of my own nameless becoming. From time to time I would leap like a salmon into the turbulent air and flash on the delineation of my condition, and find that I had transmogrified into a revolutionary, or a homosexual, or a junkie, or a heretic, or any one of the thousand things my civilization said I should not be.

I thought of the reactions of the several people who had learned of the pregnancy. 'Oh,' they said, 'a baby! How wonderful.'

There must have been an age, perhaps only in fantasy, when the birth of a child was in the natural order of things and was as much a cause for joy as the first sprouting of the winter crop in the spring. But the crops were now heavily dosed with a poison spray, and the imminent birth of a child only served to underscore the essential horror we had all done our best to make of this world.

VI

The ocean had become too heavy for us to bear. The days of listening to its restless, pitiless changes had taken their toll on our fragmented and shallow sensibilities. Also, I was detoxifying too quickly, and I found myself smoking a great deal, almost as though my body had adjusted to a certain level of atmospheric evil, and to drop too soon into an area of fresh air provided a shock to the system. I decided to go back to the city again, leaving the others to their own devices.

I rode back on the Expressway, zipping past the impacted ugliness of Long Island into the slate grey cloud in the distance. For more than thirty miles the great miasma over New York City dominated the horizon in a virulent evocation of decay. As I got closer, and the density of concrete and steel increased, the number of buildings per unit of space multiplied, and traffic built to the choked snarl where Bruckner Boulevard meets the Cross Bronx Expressway. On the West Side Highway I watched the curve of the Hudson shore fade abruptly in the black air over the infested waters of what had once been a beautiful river.

The city was in full decline. It merely needed its Hogarth to capture the idiosyncratic manner in which it festered. From day to day one wondered how it could survive another twenty-four hours: the filth in the streets, the constant screech of the cars and buses and trucks, the insane hustling from nowhere to nowhere of the grey-skinned people. The place was run by a hostile amalgam of racial power groups, construction companies, finance and transportation monopolies, and a laughable city government. It was like a speed-freak nightmare, and no one showed the slightest understanding of what was necessary to keep the deadly proliferation of new buildings, more cars, extra people, increased business from swamping every last vestige of humanity. And permeating everything, everywhere, the thick sulphurous air, the sickening water, the constant diet of dead food, in cans, in boxes, in frozen containers. What would come first? A plague? A war among the many furious factions? The destruction of the subways or bridges? Or just the continuation of a lifelessness that had become the style of life?

I glowed with exhilaration. I was free to prowl in the richest, most powerful, most decadent city in the country which was my jungle. I throbbed with pure perversion, the sense of singeing evil which the metropolis spawned like a culture in a test tube. I went to Lucinda's pad, one of those architectural whorehouses which squat over Central Park West, and paid my emotional dues to get past the doorman. He seemed instinctively to hate me, perhaps because of my hair and dress. The man was over sixty, decrepit, and so bored with standing in front of a revolving door for forty years that he had completely forgotten he was born free.

I began to feel sick to my psyche and remembered Francis's words as I had got on the ferry: 'You'd better bring along an extra set of filters for your mind.' After half an hour in New York, all of one's antennae are clogged

74

with confusion and hatred, and in short time you have joined the other seven million zoombies in their sense-less stumblings about the streets.

From the edge of hostility I receive from the man who sells me a newspaper, to the war in Vietnam is simply a matter of quantity. The conflict is internal with each individual as well as external in the world. The war my myriad selves carry out is mingled with the power syndrome inherent in authoritarian government structure, and neurotic anxiety translates to global conflict via the power of technology.

I reached the deepest understanding of myself when I saw that I was a clever killer ape, one of a species whose ferocity is destroying an entire planet. And while the liberal in me was horrified at the spectacular atrocities committed by the military, the observer in me pointed out that not a day went by in which I didn't kill with a thought or a gesture. The reality of hatred and violence in the simplest human regulations was clear.

Being a thoroughly conditioned and civilised monkey, I refused for a long time to admit the truth of my perception. On the one hand there were the police monkeys with weapons and prisons to ensure that I behaved; on the other was the imprint of so-called Christian conscience which had been burned into me from infancy.

But I couldn't for long escape the fact that the really cunning monkeys, the apes who run the machinery of the social world, the bankers, the statesmen, the generals, the religious leaders, the finance barons, stay where they are through brute force, via their armies and their systems of law, via their institutionalised religions, via the power of their hypnotists, the advertisers, and via the submissive nature of the vast majority of human monkeys who perform the countless daily deadening routines which keep everything going. In a flash I saw all of our history as a parade of concentration camps, regulating the lives of the inmates, and periodically warring against each other.

I showered and smoked a joint, and found myself enjoying the solitude and silence of the apartment. I remembered that I hadn't spent any time alone for months, and I decided to pass the evening by myself, getting my head straight. I took out a shoe box filled with photographs that ranged back to when I was two months old. It had pictures of me and my family, neighbourhood friends, scenes, women. As usual I began to float back into the levels of historical awareness I had about myself, remembering at what points in my life certain influences entered and how they shaped me. I was working up a pretty good memory when I came to the nude photo of Miriam. It was the first such shot I'd taken after discovering the miracle of Polaroid. Instant Grecian Urn! For she still lay there, her lips parted, her eyes unmasked, her cunt wet and dripping from the fuck we'd just finished.

I was twenty-five when I met her. I held an oppressive job as a junior editor on a two-man literary newspaper, and she was an apple-cheeked, sensitive-nippled, brilliant young girl from Sarah Lawrence. I was underpaid and worked long hours, but I was still in a career bag and took this as a step in what seemed to be the right direction. She came to work part time and we began a pleasant enough little soap opera, featuring the starry-eyed student and the esoteric businessman.

She was under five feet tall, a mouth barely large enough to get a medium-sized cock into, and an enormous globular arse. She radiated an aura of innocence which was electrifyingly erotic when I had her sprawled across the bed, her skirt hiked past the tops of her school-girl stockings and her fists clenching and unclenching with desire. When we fucked her eyes lost their air of childhood and became concentric rings of pure Aries power. She would do anything sexual as long as it was coated with a palatable literary jacket.

Our first few months were perfect. We could meet only on weekends, she lying to her parents about her location and coming to my pad in Brooklyn Heights where we embarked on forty-eight hour fuck marathons. Occasionally I visited her at the school, sleeping illegally in her room, snatching delicious sex from under the prowlings and patrollings of the campus guards, and becoming dizzy with the sweet stench of so much young articulate cunt in one place.

But at that moment in every relationship when one must decide whether to stay or go, I let lust cloud my judgement and started to have thoughts of a permanent union. Since neither of us really wanted that, but did not know how to cut loose, we began to hate each other secretly. And we began to feel the pressure from her parents. Her father was a Ph.D. historian who now worked as an assistant principal in a junior high school; her mother was a librarian. Both were, on the surface, pleasant and intelligent people, second-generation Jews who had moved to one of the Protestant-style swimming-pool ghettoes of New Jersey. As Miriam and I became 'serious', it became obvious that I would have to meet them.

They didn't like me at all. I was a gentile, I had no solid financial prospects, and I smelled like an adventurer. But they were civil.

I put on, as I was wont to do then, the costume and mask I thought would least threaten them. I made all the necessary placatory gestures, and left their home with all of us feeling that we wouldn't have to go through that again. But we had no way of knowing how naive we were.

At that time, *Stranger in a Strange Land* was making its first big impact on the American consciousness, and Miriam and I were infected with the notion of group love, although neither of us had any sense of what a complex and dangerous ground that is for us who have been sexually crippled by our civilisation. We were at the stage where we were chanelling all the frustrations, and dishonesties of the relationship into sex, with the result that our sex was reaching frantic levels. We mistook that for ecstasy.

One night, as I was sitting on the john and Miriam was crouched in front of me, sucking my cock, I looked in the mirror behind her and saw her cunt contracting spasmodically between her spread arse cheeks. Each time she got the head of my cock into her throat and gagged, her cunt clenched. As her tongue worked the length of the shaft and her head bobbed up and down and I felt the stretch of her lips to encompass the meat in her mouth, I imagined what it would be like if another man were to come up and fuck her from behind. It seemed to me that the excitement engendered in her cunt would ripple up her spine and feed the activity of her mouth, and vice versa. The image of her as a warm pulsating series of sensual apertures being fucked from many angles sent me into paroxysms of sharp pleasure, and I reached over to thrust my fingers into the moist space between cunt and arsehole, words of aggression pouring from my lips. I came volubly into her waiting mouth.

'We have to get another man,' I said afterwards.

'I don't want anybody else,' she said.

Heinlein's jargon came to the rescue. 'A water-brother,' I said, 'to expand the nest.'

Her eyes misted over. 'Oh, yes,' she said, 'that would be beautiful.'

But when we went over the names of all the men we knew, she found one reason or another to reject all of them. I grew exasperated, then angry, and we ended the discussion with her insisting that I was the only man she wanted. And then we fucked. It was one of the first times I tasted the sweet and guilty pleasure of fucking a woman who was in tears.

A few days later, however, she told me that a man had tried to pick her up on the street, and she had rapped with

78

him. 'He seemed nice,' she said. 'Maybe we can do it with him.'

My jealousy flared. 'You must really dig him,' I said.

'Well, you're the one who wants to bring another man in,' she said with one of her rare flashes of independent emotion.

I wasn't yet sophisticated enough to know the difference between active and passive manipulation, so I agreed to meet him, feeling as though I bore complete responsibility for the scene we were mounting. And the following Friday he came over.

He was a chubby black man with a soft and unobtrusive manner. His entire persona seemed to suggest that he wanted nothing from anyone, and would simply be mutely grateful for whatever crumbs fell his way. I was disarmed, and conned, although I wasn't aware of the latter. We talked for a bit, but all of my energy was involved with the sexual tensions in the room and we might as well not have been speaking English. Harry sat on a pillow, leaning against one wall, while I sat a dozen feet away, my back against the opposite wall. Miriam sat next to me, reclining against my side, her head on my shoulder.

I took a deep breath and let one hand drop on her left breast. His eyes flickered to the movement and flicked back again to a spot somewhere around the bridge of my nose. We talked some more, unintelligible sounds. My feet were sweating, and I began to rub her nipple between my thumb and forefinger. She flinched, relaxed, and let out a soft sigh. I shifted my weight under her and she slid down, simultaneously turning towards me, burying her face in my chest. With my other hand I pulled her skirt up, revealing her heavy chalk-white legs; up past her thighs to her hips, her pale blue panties causing an abrupt change in tone. Miriam made a tiny sound that might have been a 'No', but I swept past it and slipped my hand under the elastic and down the crack between her cheeks.

79

Harry watched, unmoving, and only when I slid one finger into her cunt did he come across the floor on all fours. he looked at her, and he seemed to be sniffing, like a dog at a strange object, and then suddenly his hand was alongside mine, abruptly digging into her flesh, knuckling his fingers into the wet warm crevice between her legs.

For several minutes we were lost in a silent frenzy. Miriam lay on her back, showing no response to what we were doing to her. Perhaps it was because we were doing it *to* her, using her body as fuel for our sexual intensity. We worked, oddly enough, as a team, without words, without a preconceived plan. In short order we took off her panties, her blouse, her bra, until she lay there, eyes closed and mouth pursed in apprehension, waiting. But Harry and I were fixated on breasts and cunt and arse. We didn't notice Miriam's total state. Amateurs that we were, we had no sense of the complexity of rhythm involved in a threesome, nor of how to keep the tension-relaxation cycle flowing smoothly. If we had simply stopped to find out where we were with each other, to check what we were feeling and how we were blocked, something lovely might have happened. But we pressed on, and Harry and I threw ourselves on Miriam's body, massaging, caressing, kissing, licking, sucking.

Suddenly my energy dropped, and I lost interest in what we were doing. I continued my activity, but inside myself a second level of awareness crystallised; I began to watch myself watching myself. I noticed that Harry was grabbing her cunt very hard, and I knew that that turned her off, being hurt before she was properly softened up. I got angry with him not only for mistreating her, but for destroying the delicacy of the operation. I put my hand under his and felt her cunt. She was dry. Everything was wrong. She should have been sopping at this point, writhing in unfulfilled desire, taking his cock in her mouth, twisting her pelvis in a silent supplication to be fucked. All the stereotypes were demanding to be recognised and I couldn't even manage an erection.

A spasm went through her body and she rolled over on her stomach. And the sight of her shining, white immense buttocks overcame even the mechanicalness of our actions. Harry and I caught each other staring down at her with slavering lust. My cock got hard. I straddled her thighs and prodded my way between her legs until I could feel the heat from her cunt, and then pulled her hips up to make it easier for me to penetrate. I sank slowly into her, the dryness of her cunt making my entry almost excruciating. She bit her lips, but in a minute began to lubricate. For the first time that day I flushed with a solid genital connection, but just then became aware of the man sitting at our side. An absolute stranger, and ironically, I didn't want him there. A sickening vibration swung through the room, and I felt my cock get soft. I was encrusted with confusion and I got off Miriam's limp form and sat by her side.

And Harry jumped to, without ambivalence or conscience. He had a much larger cock than mine, and I almost collapsed from fears of inadequacy as I saw him mount her and ease his tool between her cheeks and into her now wet cunt. To my horror I saw her arse move. I suppressed what I saw and dove into my negative sexual flow. I moved forward until her face was at my crotch and brought my cock against her lips. And for a few sizzling minutes, the magic happened. She let herself open and respond to Harry's fucking, and sucked at my cock with astonishing abandon. He rolled and bucked into her, making her shudder with a sort of tense pleasure while her head wobbled in response to his movement, making her mouth describe circles around my prick. The sight of black and white bodies churning into each other, the power of his male insistence and her wanton yielding, and the crushing beauty and energy of the eternal number three, whipped me into a thoughtless climax and I let the frantic sperm spill out of me and into her mouth.

And even as I saw her throat working to swallow the come, I was filled with dread. For Harry was still roaring. He pulled out and turned Miriam over and entered her from the front. He was past caring about my presence. He hooked his arms under her knees, spread her legs wide, and dived frothing into her cunt.

She cast her eyes towards me imploringly, asking for some kind of guidance. She didn't know how to respond in relation to my possible jealousy and to the fact that I had allowed, encouraged, things to get this far. She reached her hand towards me and I held it while he ground his hips into her, his arse rocking, and his back glistening with sweat. Then, terribly, I felt her fingers twitch. I knew that her awareness was leaving the point of contact she was making with me. And her hand went dead and began to slip from my grasp.

Then he arched back, made one decisive movement, and she groaned with pleasure. He had her. Her hand left mine completely and went up around his back. She wrapped her legs around him. And they were fucking. And I was dead. He started grunting as she pumped her cunt against his cock. She began that long keening wail which signals the onset of her orgasm. And then she let it all hang out, writhing against him, her tits crushed to his chest, her fingers in his hair, her toes curling in the air. He shouted once and came inside her, and her plevis jumped reflexively, three times, four times, five times, six times to his tune, and then she subsided, whispering, 'Oh God,' into his throat.

They lay there, oblivious of their surroundings, like two lovers who had at last found one another, as indeed they were, but I was too sour to bless their pleasure. 'Water brother!' I thought. 'Shit!' I thought.

They separated and became aware of my presence again.

I got up and went into the kitchen to put water on for a cup of tea. I was disgusted with both of them, with myself, with everything. He dressed, and once again seemed soft, apologetic, and awkward. I focused on his blackness, and the very things which would ordinarily seem sensual and exciting now seemed alien and threatening. I faced the fact of my prejudice, and realised that it made no difference at all. Hatred was inside me, and it didn't matter who the object of it was, whoever happened to be in my field of involvement when I felt it. He stood at the door. 'Well, so long,' he said. I turned my back on him.

Miriam lay in the next room, frightened. I sent her vibrations reinforcing her fear. I drank my tea slowly, smoked two cigarettes, and after a long time in the bathroom, went in and lay down next to her. I waited in stony silence as she made several attempts to say something. If she were a more centred woman she would either have gone to sleep or left and not worried about my private melodrama. But she was young and filled with Jewish upbringing, and was quite prepared to feel extremely guilty. The more I punished her, the more I touched her cultural cunt.

Finally she put her hand on my cock and began stroking it lightly. Finding no resistance, she began pulling on it until it was hard, and then she climbed on top of me. I let her fuck me for a very long time before I came, and immediately afterwards I fell asleep.

We didn't talk about the incident for an entire week. Harry called once and I was curt with him. I considered the matter closed and was somewhat pleased that I had seemingly suffered as little jealousy as I had. She went back to school for four days and returned on a Thursday. We fucked in the afternoon and at night we went to see *Rashomon*.

When it came to the husband's version, I began to get uncomfortable. And when the scene flashed showing him

83

tied to a tree, looking down as the rapist fucked his wife, I began to sweat. The camera shifts to the rapist's back, the wife's hands beating against the rough cloth of his shirt. Gradually she hits him more softly, then stops. Her fist opens, and very very gently her fingers extend and just rest lightly on his back. The delicacy of the description took my breath away, and in a flash the awful feeling of abandonment I had felt when Miriam's hand slipped from mine returned full force. I turned to her and saw her staring at me, wide-eyed. My face screwed up in anguish.

'YOU CAME!' I shouted at the top of my lungs, scaring all the other people in the theatre.

If I had been ready to recognise that the instinct to plunder is a mark of man, I would have used Miriam for what I wanted and, when I was bored, dropped her, or come to terms with the exploiter in myself and stopped using my energy to pretend I was an angel. So I could neither continue smoothly along the path to sexual cynicism, nor break through into honest confrontation. Like so many before me at this particular crossroads, I toppled over into a futile effort to attain respectability. I decided that we should get engaged, regularise our relationship, tell her parents we were in love and sleeping together, have her come live openly with me in the city each weekend, and prepare for marriage upon graduation. She thought it was a bad idea, but let herself be persuaded.

'I'm tired of sneaking around,' I said, 'I'm not ashamed of anything we're doing. We should tell your parents.'

'You don't know my parents,' she said.

'Oh, I know they're prejudiced,' I said, a bit too glibly, 'but, after all, they're educated people. They ought to be happy to have their child tell them the truth about things. They may not like your fucking me, but they should prefer that to your lying to them.'

And so, on Friday the thirteenth, we rode to Jersey, past the oil refineries and the pork processing plants, to play out the drama of confrontation. It might have been obvious to an outside observer that I was in the way of punishing Miriam and her parents, and inflicting some form of penance on myself. We had dinner, exchanging polite hostilities, and I listened to a long Semitic tirade on the evils of mixed marriages. They didn't know specifically what was about to happen, but were stringing barbed defences just on general principles.

'We have something to tell you,' I said, over after-dinner coffee.

'Oh dear,' her mother said.

I smiled. 'Miriam and I are sleeping together,' I said, 'and . . .'

But I never got a chance to go on. Her father clenched his teeth and the fingers of his right hand closed spasmodically, crushing the napkin he was holding. Her mother turned chalk white and stiffened. Then she retched violently, jumped from the table, and ran down the hall to the bathroom where she heaved up the evening's meal in great voluble gushes.

A merciful numbness enveloped me. Miriam also copped out by cauterising all connections to her emotions. Her father looked down the hallway several times, embarrassment softening his face. Having his wife's sexual hangups so pointedly and publicly exposed must have been excruciating for him. I wondered what it must be like to fuck her.

The next four hours were a pastiche of Old Testament angst with Freudian undertones of smut. Unfortunately, no one in the room was alert enough to observe passively the goings-on, to watch them with interest and wonder. We all got caught up in our performances, and the air grew thick with recriminations, accusations, and tears.

'But aren't you happy we were honest enough to tell you?' I found myself saying over and over again. They kept looking at me as though I were a plague carrier.

By midnight it was clear that they were in for an all-nighter, and both parents wanted to have a go at Miriam without my interference. The father drove me to the bus stop. He was in a state of frozen calm. 'You realise that you have totally destroyed our lives, don't you?' he said. By that time I was almost ready to believe I had. 'Excuse me,' I said. 'Sarcastic bastard,' he said. 'I'm being very sincere,' I said, 'I really feel bad.' He lost his cool. 'Feel bad!' he thundered and took his eyes off the road to lash at me with a glance of hatred. 'I ought to kill you.'

I rode back to the city without thinking, took a cab to my pad, and fell asleep with my clothes on. At six in the morning, the phone rang. It was Miriam. Her father was standing in the middle of the basement floor, tearing his hair and ripping his clothes, destroying the family Bible page by page, and wailing, 'My little girl . . . we were going to put her name in the book on her wedding day . . . oh my sweet little girl . . . my innocent little girl . . . oh my precious little darling . . . and now she's ruined . . . my little girl is dirty all over.'

'What am I going to do?' she asked after she had described the proceedings.

I wasn't awake long enough to have put on a set of cushioned responses, and the words came out spontaneously. 'Let him scream,' I said. 'It's probably the first time in years that he's felt anything at all.'

I heard a hassle on the other end of the line, and Miriam's mother broke in. 'Please,' she begged, 'I don't care about what happened. Just promise you won't do it again.'

'Do what again?' I asked.

'Oh,' she moaned, and burst into a fit of crying. 'Just don't . . . make . . . love . . . to her again.'

'You're crazy,' I said.

Another period of confused sounds, and Miriam's voice. 'Promise her, please,' she whispered. 'Just say it, so she'll

86

stop suffering so much.'

'Well,' I thought, 'so much for the people who think that higher education is some solution to the world's problems.' Here was a mother blackmailing her daughter with anguish, just to keep her from some simple fucking. 'All right,' I said, 'tell her I promise. But I tell you I'm not promising any such thing.'

It was two weeks before Miriam would fuck again, and the first time was in the midst of tears, begging her mother's forgiveness between gasps of pleasure. As she spread her legs to let me enter a deeper part of her cunt, she re-lived all the emotional upheaval of that night. It was a strange experience to fuck a woman who was in the throes of hysteria.

Afterwards, she confided that her mother had told her she would never have sex with her father again. 'Every time I even think about it,' she said 'I picture you in *his* arms.'

'Well, why doesn't she just fuck me herself?' I said, and Miriam burst into tears again.

The relationship was over. There was no way to continue with even a pretence of affection. We continued for another month, hating each other for the inevitability of the pain we were causing each other. Our sex became more freaky. The sadism and masochism which had been merely stylistic now lost all its grace. Until the last time we fucked. It ended with my pissing on her in the shower, then dragging her to the kitchen floor, shoving a coke bottle up her cunt and a broomstick up her arse, while she grovelled at my crotch and licked my balls. Finally I yanked her head back by grabbing a fistful of hair, and jerked off into her stretched mouth. As soon as the come spilled onto her tongue and she swallowed it with exaggerated motions of distaste, the bond between us was severed.

'I think it's finished,' I said.

'Me too,' she said. And she dressed and left.

Vacuums in the void wonder at the slip of silk on thigh. All the moods washing like wind through the undifferentiated atom of all atoms excreting self-conscious illusions whose profundity evaporates before the kindergarten notions of time and space.

What of the priest who followed the alarmed and holy altar boy to the spot where a consecrated wafer had fallen some days earlier?

'Look,' said the lad, 'Jesus' body lying in the dust.'

The fifty-year-old man picked it up, sniffed it, and popped it into his mouth. 'Potato chip,' he said, and destroyed Catholicism in a stroke.

I finished with the photos and stretched out on the bed, a familiar tingling and tightening in my groin. Every moment we lived was another photograph; each breath was another nail in the coffin of permanence. We ended before we began, and life was a mockery of all aspiration. The letter from the abortionist lay on the night table, and I wondered whether there was any point in taking the life of the foetus seriously. Even if it were born, it would only have to suffer through the meaningless and terrifying round of daily life, and then die, going back to nothingness whence it came. Why disturb it in the first place? To destroy it would be to destroy nothing at all. Although I seemed to remember reading somewhere, or hearing somewhere, that life was sacred. Was that another pious notion, akin to the belief in continuity? How did it stand up in the face of countless light-years of ordered chaos surrounding the petty speculations of the fragile, limited, and temporary minds of fearful manwomankind?

There was nothing for my mood but self-abasement. I went down to the Village and prowled the area between Sheridan Square and the Women's House of Detention. At three in the morning the dregs of the pervert underground flaked off from their failed scenes and congregated at the Twin Brothers coffee shop, or the corner of Eighth Street and Sixth Avenue. I found a tall unshaven blond leather boy leaning against a building. We did business with our eyes. I approached him. 'Are you interested in size?' he asked. 'Sure,' I said, 'why not?' He had a nine-inch cock which he forced again and again into my throat as I knelt before him in one of the darkened hallways of the unfortunate planet Earth.

VII

I drove out of the city at five in the morning. The muggers had called it a night and most of the skulkers had cleared the streets an hour earlier. The garbage men were invading by the thousands, their clanking tank trucks thinning out through the predawn silence. The air was as wholesome as the inside of a chimney.

When I got back Lucinda was still asleep, and Francis and Bertha were having breakfast on the sun deck. On the island, it was a golden morning.

'Have one,' Francis said, holding out a reddish-brown tablet. It was mescaline. I downed it with a sip of orange juice and sat down with them.

In the years I had known Francis, his relationship with women always followed the same pattern, a starburst meeting; a highly articulate and intense courtship filled with psychic flowers and sexual sensitivity; and a broad sweep of her mind with his magnificent loft, his books and records, his paintings, his prominent friends, his endless metaphysical rap. For a while he would ride high on the energy released from his fusion with her, and always she would make the error of assuming that at last she had found the man of her secret dreams.

Then the money would run out, and she would have to go out to work, while he excused himself on the grounds that he was working on some compelling project. Only too anxious to support a genius, she would go out to earn the necessary bread. Predictable patterns of resentment and guilt followed, and the relationship would be corroded through the friction of ill-fitting gears. He would end by deciding that she was not stable enough or sensitive enough or intelligent enough to understand him, and dispose of her in one form or another. Since he is basically a kind and good person, he would not be brutal, but wean her away slowly, paying the dues of seeing her through her changes, through her tears and fears, until she could separate herself.

His current partner in life's dance was Bertha, a twenty-three-year-old, mildly gifted photographer and painter. A Scorpio with a cunning sense of self-interest and possessiveness. Either Francis was allowing himself greater vulnerability or needed a drastic change after his previous and masochistic sculptress. Bertha was pointedly jealous of my friendship with Francis, and was entirely upfront about it.

'Perhaps after a few years, when I feel more secure with Francis, it'll be possible to let someone into our relationship in a close way. Right now I can't trust you.'

I admired her honesty but was angered by her stupidity. She had the usual female superstition that because she let a man have her cunt, she was somehow more intimate with him than a male friend of many years. Perhaps it was just my bitchiness that refused to see the way in which that was true.

'Can't you two keep the peace at all?' Francis said, playing his game of obtuseness pretending that he was not involved in the matter, trying not to let either of us see how deeply he loved the other.

94

'I grant that you're a triple Leo,' I said, 'but don't you think it's a bit presumptuous to think you can take on *two* Scorpios?'

She and I exchanged rare smiles of comradeship, the astrological tie providing a thin but implacable bond between us. I sized her up: timid, small-titted, and on the occasion I saw her naked, sporting a thin straightforward cunt. Like the rest of us, she was out for what she could get. And being a woman, that immediately involved finding a man to serve as her hitching post. On absolutely cool appraisal, I realised that the problem was my not really wanting to fuck her, except perhaps casually, her bent over a kitchen table, not bothering to take her clothes completely off.

'If you weren't such a silly little bitch,' I said, 'You'd realise that I am as much a shield as an intrusion.'

She thought about it for a moment. She smiled. 'You're right,' she said, but then her eyes clouded over. She had forgotten about it almost as soon as it entered her consciousness.

The battle continued everywhere, even in the closest friendships and love affairs, even among people who had no actual cause for war. I grew weary with the spectacle of ourselves. And began to get the first mescaline rushes.

We decided to take a walk. 'Do you mind if I come?' Bertha asked. She hadn't dropped, and knew from experience that she might be resented among people who were tripping.

'I don't want you around if you're not tripping,' he said.

'Oh God, I really hate you sometimes,' she said to him.

'What the fuck,' I said, 'let her come. What difference does it make?'

I knew full well what difference it made, yet I couldn't extricate myself from the negative energy bond that had coupled the two of us. Thus secret pacts are born; we enlist others to engage in our games, to become sympathetic or complimentary to our needs and complaints, to serve us or let us serve them, to do anything so long as the contract is honoured. Where there might have been communion among people, dissension entered and we had to resort to communication. And when the faculty of communication all but disappeared from the species, the mode of contact became complicity. To be honest in any human relationship, especially in marriage, has become a matter of two people holding loaded guns to one another's heads and negotiating from there.

The three of us set off down the beach and walked towards the Grove. When the mescaline flashes became very heavy, we stopped to lie down under a lean-to which someone had put together of driftwood and logs. Bertha went off by herself. Stretched out on our backs, Francis and I drifted into a silent mutual reverie, each feeling his own ecstasy, yet letting the waves of wonder wash back and forth freely from mind to mind, from body to body. It was a high and pure form of relating, a rarified sharing, something I have never experienced with a woman.

'Dig the Sistine Chapel,' Francis whispered.

Because we knew one another's heads so well, a few words were enough to open an entire era. The Renaissance came to life.

'Michelangelo,' I said. And the wonder of his genius shimmered in our awareness.

'Do you know what da Vinci called him?' Francis said. *'That stonecutter.'*

Understanding at once the consummate supremacy of da Vinci, and the warm iciness involved in being able to put down, with inner justification, a man of Michelangelo's scope, overwhelmed us, and we broke up in giggles. Many of our trips were like that, conversations in mental shorthand.

'Then there was Giotto,' he said, 'who founded the Renaissance.'

He was off on one of his favourite compulsions again, the notion that the painter's intellect is superior to that of any other artist. Once he had taken me on a ten-hour trip through the New York museums, teaching me about painting, and I learned more than I could have studying six years for a Master of Fine Arts degree. But I didn't want to go through it again, so I cut him short.

I rolled out of the hut and ran down the beach, stumbling and laughing, tumbling in the sand. I had a torn blanket over my shoulders and I picked up a pointed stick, holding it like a spear. For a moment I tripped out of context. I forgot the matrix of time and place and stood quite naked in the nowness of the then. I felt quite free and fierce. My stomach growled. My face held an expression of furious joy. And a truth was revealed to me concerning the human condition: to live one must eat, and to eat one must kill. No equivocation.

I returned to the shelter and found Francis and Bertha lying in an embrace, their hands on one another's genitals. I watched them for a while, and then she saw me standing there. A wave of hatred passed from her to me. 'You too,' I thought, 'Grab you and fuck you right here. Then stab you with my spear.' I blinked and turned away.

We went on to the Grove to get something to eat. As we approached its boundaries, I began to camp it up. Francis was even more reserved than he had been last time, and was condescending to the gay citizens, putting on a manshield for Bertha's benefit. I lapsed into an Italian accent, finding vicious pleasure in my role, in my distance. Meta-theatre was the ultimate refuge.

Francis knew what I was doing but was tied to Bertha. He got angry. 'Stop talking in dialect, man,' he said. 'What do you think you are, a madam from Naples?'

'Yes, darling,' I said. 'Do you want a good time? Or are you really satisfied with that naive stringbean hanging on your arm?' I was letting all my bitchiness show and

97

Bertha was no match for my age and experience and mescaline energy. We sat on the restaurant sun deck and ordered sandwiches. 'I have no money with me,' I said. 'I'll take care of it,' Francis said.

I went into the Sea Shack john, vamping and talking to myself. I saw my face in the mirror and was amazed. Hair brown, cheeks red, eyes flashing, lips full. I was beautiful, the way a woman can be beautiful.

'So this is what they see,' I said to the glass. 'This is what they desire, the fools who want to make love to me, who want to fuck me, to have me moan in their arms. It is the beauty they want to suck up, to feast upon. Then let them have it!'

And on saying that I looked down and found two dollar bills crumpled at my feet under the urinal. It was one of those coincidences that lend poetry to causality.

After the lunch, when the bill arrived, I threw the two dollars on the table. 'I thought you didn't have any money,' Bertha said. 'I found some,' I said, loading the words with suggestiveness. Francis was impressed, sitting at the round wooden table overlooking the ocean, his shoulder-length blond hair forming a mantle for his head, his square-cut beard the most prominent feature of his lean six-foot frame, his blue eyes sparkling in an ironic glitter, while his dinosaur-mouth girl friend breathed flames of envy over my aura.

Back at the house, things were festering nicely. Lucinda had left to see an old friend in Ocean Bay Park, and three strangers were sitting in the living room. I looked into their eyes and saw confusion. There were people everywhere, and everywhere the people had one or another game they want to suck others into, to compensate for their own emptiness. Everyone had a private plot that was projected onto the world; if you peered into their souls, you could see what sort of actors and actresses they were advertising for. I didn't mind acting in someone else's movie, but the people here were vague about their desires, they were just groping, neither open to the flow of events, nor ready to impose their will upon the flux.

'You've never seen me naked, have you?' said Donna, sidling up to me. 'Why don't you go on up to my room and wait for me there?'

'Don't forget that she is mad,' I said to myself as I climbed the stairs. 'You've never let that stop you before,' said one of my other voices.

Donna had so fused her internal fantasy life into a cutting tool for dealing and dividing up the world around her that she seemed perfectly balanced. If one stepped into her game, he would buy into a razor-slicing trip in which he was never sure whether his partner was a friend or raving enemy. I attempted to stay neutral by applauding her act each time I saw it so as to distract her from the fact that I was still outside of it.

I lay on the red shag rug, lit a stick of incense, and filled a pipe with hashish. Within a few minutes, she came in. She stood over me and arched her back, forcing her great breasts out.

'I used to be whipped by the nuns when I was eleven,' she said. 'They were jealous of my body.' And the crazy-lights went on in her eyes.

I got an erection and took off my pants, all the while watching her. She lay down next to me. 'I can't fuck you,' she said. 'I just thought it would be nice, you know, friendly, if you saw me without clothes once before the end of the summer.'

All the warning signals went off. Lucinda was still asleep. And if she woke up, she would not come up here.

'You can do anything you want with me,' I said.

She stood up and slowly peeled off her pants and blouse and brassiere and panties. She had an excellent body, but lacked the fullness of her narcissism. If she could let go, she would be one of the most sensuous women in the world.

But now it was merely curvaceous flesh, full thighs, and all the rest of it.

'Close your eyes,' she said.

The next sensation was that of her hand in a mink glove, rubbing my genitals. I began to stir. In the distance I could hear the noises of the house. Bernard and Josephine talked in the room down the hall. He was the son of Jewish refugees and now sported a doctorate in economics, and was writing a meaningless book on the statistical aspects of welfare in the United States. His wife was a lantern-jawed simpleton with a lovely arse. They always talked as though there were a surly child in the corner of the room listening to them, forcing them to some obscure form of proper behaviour.

'If you were clean, I would suck you,' Donna said.

'I'm clean,' I said.

She threw herself on her back, her legs opening. 'Oh, I can't,' she sighed, and in the same breath, 'I like men to be rough with me.'

Tedium threatened.

I considered the situation. She was clearly working out some baroque schoolgirl fantasy drama, operating on a very low level of consciousness and upset by her own directions. There could be no passion in this scene, no humour, no richness of contact. On the other hand, I felt an honest affection for her, and was quite taken by her body.

I bit her nipples, hard enough to hurt but not cause any damage. She brought her knees up towards her chest in a reflex motion. I wondered whether medical science might not add a new test to its list of knee-jerk and Babinski responses, and call it the Surrender Reflex, measuring to what degree a man or woman has all the orgasm pathways in good working order.

I climbed on her, pinning her arms with my knees, and forced my cock to her mouth. She played the conventional role, whipping her head from side to side, moaning, 'No, don't please don't,' and the rest of it. I grabbed her hair by the roots and tried to pry her mouth open with my cock. But her jaw was clamped tight, and in a few minutes I got bored with the theatre. I got up quickly, began to put my pants back on, and edged away from the bed. 'Well, Donna, it's been interesting, but I have to go.'

'Don't get angry.'

'I'm not angry.' I waited.

She snaked up off the floor and pulled me back down. 'I'll do something nice for you,' she said, and rolled me over on my back and sat on my now limp cock. 'I can't fuck now, but I'll rub against you until you come.'

And it became rather pleasant. Me lying there, Donna pressing her cunt and fleshy buttocks against my groin, the sunlight coming in through the window, and all the other crazies in the house doing their own thing. But in the midst of it all, she said, 'I hope Jack doesn't come in.'

The hairs on the back of my neck tingled. 'Jack?' I said. 'Who's Jack?'

'He's my lover,' she said, looking dreamily off into space. 'He's very jealous and he always carries a gun.'

'I warned you she was crazy,' said the mocking voice inside me. 'Now you're in for it. Paying the final price for the most idiotic act.'

'Do you think he might come in, now?' I said.

'Oh, he's probably on his way.'

I sat up. She pushed me back down. 'You're not afraid, are you?'

'No,' I lied. And lay back down. She began her motion again.

The problem now showed itself to be extremely simple: could I come before Jack did?

Donna began rapping again, a surrealistic mixture of early childhood memory and grisly stories of how Jack had beaten up men who had flirted with her, all the while

101

rubbing, rubbing her now heated cunt lips against my cock. And I realised that she wasn't in any contact with the sexual act, but with the danger, with the illicitness of things. I put in an emergency call to the gonads to speed things up, and while she whispered her garbled insanities and smiled vacuously at my squirmings, I pushed against her and urged myself on, 'Come on, hurry up, hurry up.' And finally I felt heat, the rush, and the spurt. The white sperm spilled over my pubic hair and belly.

We both froze for a moment, then I rolled out from under and got dressed very quickly. Engine whistles were going off in my mind.

She got up and we stood there for a moment. 'I hope we can really fuck sometimes,' she said.

'Sure,' I said.

Another moment of stillness. 'Well, I have to go.'

'Goodbye,' she said, standing there, naked, jiggling, mad, luscious.

Downstairs, Lucinda had returned. I kissed her and finally made the second cup of coffee. We sat on the deck for a while, smoking, watching the day put itself together. 'You were in Donna's room?' said Francis.

I glowered into my cup. 'Yeah, she wanted me to help her move her dresser.'

He raised one eyebrow. 'Oh really? She had me up there for the same reason yesterday.' I looked up and caught his eyes. Not only had I been a fool, but I was merely one in a long line. The two women exchanged glances, but Francis and I guarded all access points to our inner meaning. They could suspect, but had no handle to grab on to. I enjoyed the male camaraderie of the shared secret, and for a brief instant I felt a rare peace in just being human. The absolute clarity of the sky and soothing murmur of the waves had erased most of the insistent awareness of the grotesque parody that has come to inhabit the words 'only human'. I found myself smiling to myself, and responding to the small play of affection on Francis's mouth, and so much good feeling flooded the space that even Lucinda's and Bertha's suspicions melted, and they joined us in our moment of quilted mirth.

Where was the fear now? How quickly the circumstance changed; what had been the jagged edge of terror became a sweet sharing of love. But more often in my life, the trend had been in the other direction.

My first time in therapy began with overtures of noble humanity and ended in the emotional gutter. My therapist was a tiny woman of about forty-five, and a little too heavy to be considered anything but fat. Her approach was an eclectic grab-bag of traditional theories and avant garde techniques, with a strong neo-Reichian bias. The whole thing was submerged in great bowls of chicken soup which she dispensed as easily as advice on cold winter days.

One day, after almost a year of opening my heart to her, and letting her run all kinds of breathing and body trips on me, I looked up from some convoluted rap I was into and saw her gazing at me with lustrous eyes, warmth and affection pouring from her huge breasts. I was taken aback.

'Why, Sarah,' I said, 'you're beautiful.'

She got up and came over to me. 'Thank God,' she said, 'I thought you'd never notice.' And kissed me on the mouth.

I was shocked, and froze in the chair. I still had the romantic notion that therapy was a more sublime mode of existence than just plain life, and that a therapist was above the mundane desires which plagued the rest of us. But when she put her hand on my cock, all my evaluations dissolved and I responded emphatically to the gesture.

'Not here,' she said, 'I make it a practice never to fuck in the office.' Her words were like cold water. They stated most clearly that she did this often. But I suppressed the thought. 'I'll come to your place, later, she said.

The first fuck was so overwhelming that I didn't

experience it. Sarah was goddess and Mother Earth and the spirit of Freud and my personal ticket to salvation all in one, and when she swarmed over me with all of her bodies and minds, I blew all my fuses and lost consciousness of what I was doing. Some whispered words remain in my memory, and the feeling that the skin of our bellies had disappeared and our entrails were spilling and coiling inextricably into each other, binding us together like Siamese twins. But when she was finally lying peacefully by my side and saying, 'That was wonderful,' in my ear, I realised that I had maintained an erection and come in her without being aware of it.

For a month or so, we attempted to continue the therapy and the fucking, but sex was too strong for the fragile bonds of our professional relationship. And as soon as I ceased being her patient, the metamorphosis took place. In therapeutic sessions, if I had said, 'I hate you,' to her, she would patiently help me contact the feeling, scream it or kick it out, and then examine the aspects of its causes and contingencies. But once we became pure lovers, any expression of negative feeling on my part was taken as a personal attack on her, and she would get sullen or hurt. She lost all objectivity concerning the fact that I had a right to my feelings, and would whine, 'Why do you hate me? Please don't hate me.'

I began to feel oppressed, and this was the prelude to introducing violence into sex. I found I could no longer share my fantasies with her, and their energy emerged in ugly forms. Perhaps she had her own guilt concerning what she was doing, but she readily fell into the masochistic posture necessary to complement my rage. It was with her, for the first time, that I saw myself slapping a woman.

I was only twenty-four, and although she became the victim physically, I suffered immense psychic damage. One fuck had me pouncing on her again and again as she tried to crawl away from me across the floor and over the furniture. I finally pinned her to the couch and fucked her in the arse, growling in the cavern of her soundproof studio. I bit her neck and became the leopard killing the deer. I gnawed on her skull and became the caveman cannibal. Her eyes filled with a watery pleading which oscillated between wanting to let go and wanting to be totally brutalised. Her whimpers inflamed me. I wanted not only to kill her, but to eat her, to tear her flesh and swallow it, the blood running down the corners of my mouth.

'Do you want coffee?'

Lucinda was standing over me. Francis looked at me with an expression of puzzled amusement.

'What's happening in your head?' he said.

Lucinda seemed tired. I put my arms around her waist and rested my cheek against her belly. I felt her stiffen, and then relax. She stroked my hair. I held her arse in my hands.

We cleared the breakfast dishes and went into town, to make the rounds of post office, newspaper, supermarket, and coffee shop. The simplicity and ease of the routine always charmed me. Warm weather, lack of automobiles, and limited population were all it took to keep civilisation pleasant.

'They are destroying the world,' said Francis.

I looked up. He and Bertha were a few steps in front of us, hand in hand. Lucinda and I walked in steps, but not touching. For once the arrangement did not anger me. I found myself enjoying the pattern we formed, each male and female mated, and the couples forming a loose nucleus.

'Nobody seems to mind,' I said.

The four of us stopped at once. The sun was behind a bank of clouds and its ray fell in a perfect fan over the entire bay. The edges of the clouds were silver, and the dense middle sections black from their own shadow. Several sailboats chased a capricious breeze, and the whole earth was vibrant with the thunder of light.

105

'Classic!' said Francis.

'A *New Yorker* cover,' I said.

'That's a decadent association,' said Lucinda.

A lively tune played in her eyes, and her mouth was still raw from the dreams of the night before. She wore a long cotton dress which gave her the appearance of long walks in the pine forest. Some slight chemical transformation changed our levels of energy, and all at once I found myself digging her quite openly and frankly, delighting in her presence, in her person. She smiled, and then became embarrassed. She took my hand and looked away, then looked back, saw my eyes still on her, and threw her arms around my neck.

I let myself accept the possibility of union. I thought of Dante G. swimming lazily in his private pool, and an unexpected explosion of joy staggered me. The miracle of love and birth became real right before me. It seemed that I had only to say yes, and all of it would be possible.

'But like the *New Yorker* cover,' Francis said, 'it's illusory. Fire Island is where the Wizard of Oz lives. Over in Cherryless Grove. They've gone too far. It's nuclear weapons, or nerve gas, or a simple accumulation of poison. Give it, say, fifty years.'

We reached the edge of town. Outside the several bars were scores of boxes with empty booze bottles and beer cans. Cigarette butts made a mosaic on the paths. The police launch and the supply ferry were idling in the dock, farting black and blue clouds of exhaust in the air. The stores kept a brisk trade going in and out of their doors. I went to buy some cigars. 'Fifty-five cents,' the clerk said. 'But they're only thirty-three cents in the city,' I said. 'This ain't the city,' he said.

'Those fucking thieves,' I complained to the others.

'I bought a book the other day,' said Bertha. 'A seventy-five cent book. And he charged me ninety cents. What's the other fifteen cents for? I asked him. And he said, Ten

106

cents is the charge because it's Fire Island, and the other five cents is because we can get it.'

'Did you pay?' asked Lucinda.

'I wanted the book,' Bertha said.

This was about the longest conversation the two of them had ever had. I was depressed by the structure of the formation again, and I could see nothing but limitation coming from these straight, rational, polite people. Life is not like that. Life is confusion and anger and fear; life is danger, and the ecstasy of tasting forbidden fruit. And here we were, quietly being fleeced by the rapacious merchants of a corrupt summer resort, while a world destroyed itself, and made pretty conversation across the parameters of our self-imposed strictures. I was on the brink of beginning to blame the others for the discomfort I was feeling when I remembered I had reminded myself that when the environment became inhospitable, the best thing to do was leave.

I had tried to deal with the problem through the 'work it out' approach, but at certain points only solitude heals. This was one of them. And yet I didn't want to be physically alone, merely to be with people who allowed me to come out of myself as much as I wanted, and demanded no more. I felt a paradoxical mixture of excitement and withdrawal within myself, a sort of turned-on passivity. It was the mood of homosexual fucking, which was coming to seem less an end in itself than a corrective for the impossible tensions of male-female relationship. Even the purity of the homosexual act had been corrupted.

'I'm going for a walk,' I said. And as I strode away I saw the look of hurt in Lucinda's eyes. But there was nothing to say.

VIII

As I knelt in the sand, the sun sprinkling through the bay leaves, the two men in front of me pulled their cocks from the tops of their bathing suits and dangled them in front of my mouth. They embraced and began kissing, deeply, wetly. I took a deep snort of the popper and opened my lips wide to let both organs in. One of them was dark and thin, perhaps some five inches long, while the other was practically chalk white with an orange head, the kind of cock that flushes thick and full from the base eight inches to the tip. The silken heads rubbed against the top of my mouth and the inside of my cheeks, while I slipped my tongue sideways between them, making a cushion for their thrusts. Another man came up behind me and slipped off my bathing suit, then fucked me with one of those seven-eighths erections which are so tantalising.

I had returned to the house, picked up the remains of a box of amyl nitrate, some hash, a towel, and walked to the meat rack, the stretch of woods between Cherry Grove and the Pines. Cruising in the woods provided a keen pleasure that freshened the senses and elevated the soul. Here the crucial element of the hunt came into focus, and sex became largely secondary, the eating of the food which has already been killed. But it was the chase and the kill which captured the imagination of the body.

Barely discernible paths winding through thirty acres of thick brush and small trees, with unexpected clearings, and openings onto the dunes. Behind a tree, one man leaning against the bark, the rough wood scratching his back, as another performed the time-hallowed rite of cocksucking. In a hollow behind a tuft of grass, five men in tableau, their limbs and heads in an intricate and artificial tangle. Leather boys lurking in the bushes, and bikinied queens peddling their arses behind the poison ivy.

For now, there was the silent struggle and sensation of four men in a spontaneous but oddly well-rehearsed sexual act: the two men above me in communion through their kisses and deriving energy from the heat of my mouth on their cocks; the man behind me sopping up the pleasure of cock-in-arse and the sweet voyeuristic delight of the churning flesh in front of him. It was more of a dance than a fuck. For one thing, most of the people cruising did not have ejaculation as a primary goal, but wanted as many physical *contacts* as possible. So there was no passion here, no sense of intimacy or warmth, although we went through the paces of the closest act possible.

We moved together until we seemed to reach some sort of consensus. No one had a physical climax, there was no ejaculation, but rather a sense of accomplishment, of completion. The two men in front of me pulled up their suits and walked away, while the man behind me pulled out abruptly. I turned to my left and saw that three more men were standing there; they had been quietly watching the action. I was surrounded by a row of cocks. My knees were weak and I was breathing hard. I felt giddy. 'Well, why not?' I thought, and took another hit from the inhalator. The drug loosened me up even more and I went for the black in the middle. It was already throbbing and

112

the length of it slid easily down my throat. The man to whom it was attached began sucking in air through his teeth and his legs buckled.

Then, 'Take it baby,' he said, and pushed the head of his cock against the roof of my mouth. And splashed his sperm against it, causing the fluid to run straight down my throat and drip on the back of my tongue. I put all my attention on the taste, texture, and symbolism of moment, for this, theoretically, was the point of my endeavours. I swallowed without closing my lips, and got a flash on the suggestive picture my face must have presented just then, the gulping open mouth, the closed eyelids, the straining upward posture, and the glistening black cock sliding out past the lips, leaving a thin trail of pearly fluid.

He too turned quickly and left, and one of the others moved in on me. There was something about this vibration that made me look up, and I saw the closed brutal face of a man without humour or intelligence. He totally lacked the understanding that everything happening in the woods was a game, and like any game, depended on delicacy for its success. Even degradation was possible, so long as each actor understood that the essential dignity of the other had to be respected. The glorious thing about the meat rack was that much of the finding and losing took place on the basis of mental projections. I stood up and brushed past the man. He grabbed my wrist. I could read the hurting lust in his eyes and for an instant almost felt sorry enough for him to go down again. But I was tired of the sport and left.

Smoking hash along an empty stretch of beach, I played back the past few hours. Why was it that the sense memory of baby was so often associated with the sharpest moments of sex? When I am ranged over a moaning woman and at the height of ecstasy she cries, 'Oh baby,' and when I am on my back and a great cock is sending shivers of cunt

113

through my cheeks and bowels, the man above me shouts, 'Oh baby,' I wonder at the implications of the word. Certainly, when sucking a cock and gagging on its head I often felt like a baby being force-fed. In fact, the more I whimper and try to push it away, the more exciting the deed becomes for the man who is doing it to me. Perhaps much of fucking is a vain attempt to revive patterns left incomplete since childhood.

When all these *recherché* aspects of sex are neutralised, what is left, and why do we continue to fuck?

When fuck is intransitive, then the act becomes as routine as eating: I eat with you, I fuck with you. When it is used transitively, and the sense changes to 'I fuck you,' the theatre of personality opens and the drama of our intercourse overshadows all the excitement of the actual sensations.

The human race may have moved to the status of *homo promiscuans*. What keeps me from any experience except the fear grown in the hotbed of conditioning? All values which have come to us from the past are worthless unless we rediscover the state which gave rise to them, and only then can we truly decide whether to maintain them as values. We must break all the commandments which are a priori laid on our heads.

When I went to court to pay the fine, I realised that this so-called civilisation operates at the level of a dimwitted Protestant school teacher. We sat in chairs set up in rows. We were glowered into silence by a foot-tapping policeman. And when our names were called we had to walk up to the desk, lower our heads, and explain why we did such a naughty thing. It was interesting that the fines were lower in direct proportion to the tone of whining in the defendant's voice. The more abject, the more sorry one was, the more magnanimous the judge became.

Fascism is nothing but the acculturation of self-deception.

'I'm not alienated,' Francis once said. 'I'm just the latest model of a line in an evolutionary experiment. Consciousness is only a tool, part of the design. The whole Krishnamurti trip of anguished solitude is romantic horseshit.' Yet I seem to wage an unrelenting war against encroachment on my individuality. One day Lucinda and I got on the ferry and she said, 'Where shall we sit?' And I flashed paranoia and thought, 'Why *we*? Who made this unconscious assumption of *we*?'

I walked down the beach, wondering at the stream of murky analysis churning through my mind. To my left lay a hundred and eighty degrees of ocean horizon, the sky a thousand shades of blue and grey, the green and violet and pink-tinged water, the almighty sun. Sandpipers and seagulls skirted the shore. And every five or ten minutes, another person passed. We would smile, and perhaps say a few words, show one another the rocks and shells we had picked up. Each time I was taken by how uncomplicated it was to relate to a stranger, and how dense interactions became when expectation, the daughter of desire, entered the scene.

A model of three forces suggested itself to describe what happens between two people. At any time we are a function of distance, uncertainty, and complexity; and the fitness of a relationship depends on whether the product of these forces remains a constant. Thus, if there is a great distance between two people – including psychic or emotional or temperamental as well as physical distance – the degree of uncertainty and/or complexity would have to be low. If both distance and uncertainty were large, then complexity would have to be reduced almost to zero if the relationship were to continue successfully.

I wasn't sure whether what I was thinking made sense, and yet I realised that it was as arbitrary to assign the label 'electron' to an energy manifestation as to consider 'complexity' a unit of relationship. It seemed that the proper psychology would turn out to be a poetry of structural appearances.

The problem with marriage, or any fixed long-term relationship, was that habit petrified uncertainty at a single point, distance was shrunk by fear and not allowed its healthy fluctuation, and as a result complexity proliferated past the ability of the people to keep up with the changes. The result was exhaustion, with its sniping, temporary truces, futile impulses to escape, and all the trappings of a long unpopular war.

The role of sex was usually to distort the true appraisal of the actual distance between partners, so that two people could feel quite close when in fact their fucking had them flying apart at astonishing speeds.

Eric and Suzanne had had just that problem.

When I knew him he was working part-time in one of the millions of offices in downtown Manhattan while studying for his doctorate in political science. Suzanne was a secretary, a French Jew with a tight mouth and a morbid fear of impropriety. Eric fell in love with her arse, which was subtly mounded and stood out nicely from her small compact body. Each day he waited for glimpses of Suzanne's arse, watching her as she walked and sat and bent over to pick things up. On the evenings when I saw him, in the midst of a thick rap, he would say, 'There's this chick at the office, and she has the most beautiful arse.' All the while he maintained a civilised surface relationship, going through the mandatory gestures of polite intercourse.

After a few weeks he asked her out to dinner and a movie, and found her a pleasant girl to be with. They found a number of tastes in common, and shortly he was embroiled in infatuation and romance. She reciprocated. They began to talk about living together. They fucked a dozen or so times, enough to be sure that there were no hideous sexual discrepancies. And in the process of all this, he forgot what it was that was driving him, the fixation

116

no resistance as he pushed her back on a couch, lifted her skirt, and slid his cock into her very wet cunt. He turned his friends on to the Phenomenon, and she shortly became the resident pincushion of SNCC's One Hundred and Twenty-Fifth Street office.

It took Eric a few months to learn about it, not from any external evidence, but from sensing the internal changes in her. As she pulled further away from him, his emotional involvement with her heated up. He even regained his lust for her. But his heart wasn't in it. And when one morning she returned from a night of being steadily fucked by five of freedom's young stalwarts, all Eric could manage was a convulsion of self-pity.

She left that afternoon, and two days later he snapped to, went to the Y for a steam bath and a swim, ate a steak dinner, and got soaringly drunk on cold tap beer. He was out of the bag he had sewn himself in. It had taken two years.

Is the hole more than the sum of its hearts? A cunt and cock can interact, but can a man and a woman relate? Two dykes walked along the beach, one soft and brown, like a soul sloop, the other thrusting and blonde, the sighted land. In the eyes of the second was a fierce pride, a lonely painful joy, and with such sure intelligent understanding of exactly what kind of thing the two of them were that I felt a pang of envy. But perhaps in a few hours they would be sniping at one another with well-adjusted missiles of hatred.

The couple is the insignia of civilisation rampant, which has pulled war, exploitation, dense stupidity, and lies from its historical sleeve. The casual logic is implacable. For some false concept of relationship, some erroneous notion of what a family is, have come the good citizens, the upright parishioners; the fodder for convents and armies, the grease for the bears of civil law. The marchers, the boosters, the flag-wavers, the voters, the workers in the factories of the rulers, who send their children to the regimented schools, who dress the same, eat the same, have no thoughts except the reflexes patterned by the concerted conditioning of millennia.

At the meeting, the militant homosexual stood up and demanded his right to serve in the army.

When fags want to go to war, the murder of the foetus achieves a new dimension. If it could survive, if it had a world to come into, there might be some cause for joy. But its mother is a tired and passive woman who knows no other form of relationship to a man than to sink into his shadow. And its father is embarked on some mad experiment to relive all the animal archetypal historical forms through the use of his organ and orifices.

While the four of us had performed our ritual, sucking and fucking in suspended silence, the only sounds being the sighs of slippage and suction, I became the essence of a pig, wallowing in dirt, eating what no one else will touch, looking with inward-turned eye at the foolishness of the two-legged ones who are forever shooting noises out of their mouths and indulging in silted pantomimes of behaviour they really don't want to take part in. In utmost realism then, I saw that the world will ever be ruled by the stunned insensate, by the worthless and the petty and the mean. From Rameses to Nixon, a line of bestial mediocrity. And there is no chance that the species will change it ways. The governments of the world will continue to exemplify and magnify the violence, greed, ignorance, and unswerving hostility to all forms of sexual love which have proven the identifying marks of manwomankind throughout recorded time.

There is nowhere on the horizon of macrocosmic social events the slightest glimmer of intelligence, the faintest hope for sensitivity to the nature of reality. We have become nuclear lemmings, racing for the final cliff, and the most articulate among us can do nothing but sound the klaxons of doom or else attempt to further hypnotise the populace and their leaders into believing that it is all business as usual.

And before the execution of the monsters who run the states which are entered into the final unholy war, look in the mirror and see the face of the one who still says love when he means possession, who still pretends that it is possible to claim the body and affection of another human being to the utter exclusion of every one else on the surface of the planet. Look into the eyes of the one who holds the knife to his unborn child's throat and with a welter of rationalisations pushes the point forward and dispatches that life with all the efficiency of a jailor executing a political prisoner.

A man approached across the sand. He was almost sixty, but his body was still firm. He had a white goatee and wore a golfer's cap. He should have been wearing knickers.

He cruised me to a halt. I stopped, through sheer surprise. And he launched us into the ritual of proposition. As I said the necessary words, I calculated my measure of fleshly desire. Nothing came through. He didn't excite anything in me.

'Don't you find me the least bit attractive?' he asked when I was forced to remove his hand from my breast.

'With me,' I said, 'it's a matter of chemistry. It's nothing personal. If I had felt a spark I wouldn't care how old you were, or how ugly.'

'I'm only fifty-seven.'

'Please,' I pouted, 'do not make me sad.'

'At least take a walk with me,' he said, 'into the woods.'

'Don't torture yourself,' I said. But he made a gesture, an almost inward movement, and for the length of a hesitation I felt an attraction to him. It passed quickly, but not before he had slipped under the curtain and began to lead me by the arm towards the dunes. In deference to the

121

deftness of his action, I let myself be guided. He handled me with amazing grace, and I felt like a great lady being escorted across the ballroom to meet the count. My heart fluttered and the tiniest wave of faintness made me trip.

'Be careful,' he said.

I looked at him. Suddenly I saw myself as this foolish young man being taken to the woods to be fucked by this accomplished melancholy satyr. I began an internal resistance.

He did a fairly good job of maintaining some shreds of elegance while he peered eagle-eyed for a private spot. He took me behind a clump of bushes. We could not be seen. I was angry. He reached for my shoulder. 'I told you to save yourself the trouble,' I spat at him. But I sat down.

He was tender. He reached behind me and broke off a stalk from the plant growing there. He crushed it between his fingers. He held it up for me to smell. I was catapulted back to childhood. 'It's the base for sarsaparilla,' he said.

He told me the names of all the things growing there, and said he was a botanist, and held my hand and looked at me with absurdly serious eyes. He reached forward to kiss me. Unaccountably, I was repulsed. His mouth twitched.

'I'm really very sorry,' I said. He struggled to hold me down, but I stood. I turned. I let him look at my arse, at the pleasure treasure he wanted and would not have. I wanted to hurt him, with pins. He clutched my calf. I shook him off. He grabbed at my wrist. I began to move off, dragging him.

'Don't make a scene,' I thought.

I stopped. He looked up, dog-eyed. Then, mustering all his dignity in a swoop, he raised himself to one knee, bent his head forward in the military manner, and kissed my hand, I threw my other hand up to my forehead, the knuckles in a vertical line above the left eyebrow. I let him kiss my fingers and my palm. He inserted his tongue into

122

the centre of my palm. I felt ravished. Symbolic fucking
had its own forms of virginity. He squeezed my hand one
time, and let it drop. I walked over the dunes, back onto
the beach, blushing furiously, hoping no one had seen me,
was now looking at me.

'One may *always* escape into metatheatre, Francis; the
new paradigm is here, demanding its worship.'

He looked up from his book. 'Explain?' he said.

Lucinda came into the room. I told her the story of what
had just happened with the old man. She clapped her hands
in delight. It was one of those moments when I am
surprised to find a woman understanding the metaphysic
of my message when even so perspicacious a man as Francis
misses the point. For an instant I almost grasped a key to
unlock the mystery of the sexes. It was not a question of
superiority of inferiority, but of quality of perception, an
angle of being. The door to the insight slammed shut.

'Metatheatre, eh?' Francis said.

'Why not metamovie?' Lucinda added.

'Metahologram,' I concluded.

The two women and I sent happy vibrations of shared
vision dancing through the air.

'It doesn't grab me,' Francis said. 'Historically, we are
in a period of a-history. Interface space. You are basically
reductionist in your appreciation of reality. Truth
subsumes all attempts to understand it. An epochal
paradigm has to be comprehensive.'

'Fuck Bucky Fuller,' I said.

'Krishnamurti sucks,' he said.

'Why did you leave that way?' Lucinda asked. We were
back in the bedroom. 'Don't you like me at all?'

'It's more complicated than that,' I said.

'Make it simple,' she said.

'What difference does it make?'

She stopped, almost caught in the swirl of dialogue, and
then latched on to her emotion again. 'Don't you care at

123

all?' she said.

'I care. But living with you is another matter.'

'I'm not sure I want to live with you either,' she said.

'The rent's paid until the end of the summer. There's no reason why we can't live in peace, and separate then. But you keep holding on now because you know you are going to have to let go in the future.'

'Oh, you are a bastard,' she said, killing me with the words.

'Fuck you,' I said. 'Don't try to make me feel guilty for not being what you think I ought to be.'

'If it weren't for the baby, it would all be manageable,' she said.

I took a breath. 'If you have it, I'll come live with you for short periods of time each year. That's all I can or want to do. Now the decision is yours.'

'You're no man,' she spat at me.

'And are you a woman?' I said.

We were back at the impasse. 'The only consolation,' I added, 'is that no one else seems to be any better.'

I went to root around in the kitchen. I ate and went back into the bedroom. She was lying naked on the bed. She had been crying and now looked extremely beautiful.

'Fuck me,' she said, softly, 'make love to me.'

As I took her in my arms she laughed wildly. 'After all, there's no chance I'll get pregnant,' she said.

IX

How many lovers lie awake alone this night?

This is not the most vital consideration in this world of pain. Take aspirin, take television. Forget. But who cares? And when one cares, the sufferer clings to her with hatred for her concern. Cover me over, don't show my shame. Neurotic pursuits into the midnight mind. Betrayal is epidemic, as unnoticed as breathing.

'He used to come over to screw me once a week,' Lucinda said.

'I don't want to hear about it,' I shouted.

She never spoke about her sexual past again.

'Why don't you ever talk about yourself?' I said. She couldn't win. I had hurt her. She took me at my word, she obeyed me.

She went back to the city again, disconsolate this time, with something of the air of the child who must leave the playground feeling that the others would really prefer to be without her. It was a chillingly rapturous September morning as she stepped onto the ferry, crisp and yellow with sunlight. I remembered the years of buying new pencil boxes and notebooks in the bittersweet preparations for returning to school. During the night I had dreamt that Francis and I were locked in a room with a swimming pool, guarded by a mad nun.

'I really don't want to go back to the city,' she said.

'Then don't go.'

'You don't want me here.'

'I don't want you in my immediately physical vicinity, but it's a big house and a big island.'

She preferred her hurt to my logic. 'I'll go see a movie,' she said. I heard the desolation in her voice, and I didn't care. There was no malice in my mood, it was just that her wound did not reach the area of my concern.

'This is what it is like to be a monster,' I thought.

Perhaps it was this coldness which triggered her bouts of parasitism. I did not love her. And her soul growled with hunger. Once, when I was fucked by a stranger, he kept holding back his sperm, refusing to come, riding his sensation to the peak and sliding back. I grew desperate. My arse became a cunt became a vacuum, sucking at him, stuttering into him. Of course, he was delighted, this was just the effect he wanted, the pleading of the flesh for more penetration. At one point a surge of magnetic desire swept me by surprise, and caught him unawares. The sperm flew from him before he could catch himself. He froze in anger as his cock throbbed into me, and then he reared back and slapped me hard across the face. 'You dirty bitch,' he said. I was stung, but inside myself I smiled in triumph.

That sweet smile of victory-in-defeat was something Lucinda's Jewishness did not allow either of us to have. But it was an expression that had been burned eternally into my memory through Beverly, whose madness had made my twenty-third year on this planet almost my last.

I had been living with her and George and Julia in a welter of confused communality and exuberant Marxism in a Brooklyn brownstone. She moved in with me after we had spent a night burning the ends of one another's hair

128

with butane cigarette lighters. Her round face shone with imbecile intelligence and I couldn't stop shivering. Our fucking was superb. She was hanging out all the time. Her body was firm from dancing, breasts barely larger than a handful each, a perfect arse, and a rich cocoa skin. Touching any part of her was like touching cunt. Her mind swung from brilliance to stupidity with startling ease. She was also suicidal.

After her third attempt, I moved out. It was the night that George and Julie and I came home to find the house smelling of gas, blood over the kitchen walls, and my clothes and books in a torn scatter across the living room floor. We searched in horror for her body, but she was gone. The next morning I split before anyone else was awake.

'Well, where are you?' said George when I called him.

'I'm at a friend's house,' I said.

'Comrade, this is irresponsible,' he said, calling upon the Socialist conscience we were supposed to be sharing.

'Look, man,' I said, 'last week she came to bed with a knife and spent three hours muttering to herself. And I was afraid to get up and I couldn't go to sleep, and I had to just lie there, you know, just staying awake, until she finally conked out. Maybe with me gone she won't be so crazy. Maybe you can take care of her.'

'ME?' he shouted, with visions of what an International would really be like suddenly piercing his consciousness.

But just a few weeks after installing myself in another friend's pad, retribution struck. I had the place to myself for the evening and had invited Alice over, a strange girl who dug being whipped with army shirts that had metal buttons. We had just reached the point where glances were taking the place of words, when the phone rang. Ordinarily, at such moments, I ignore electronic intrusions, but on a whim I picked it up. It was Beverly. She was crazy again, and had somehow learned my number.

'I'm at George's,' she said. 'I'm coming over there.'
'But you can't know my address,' I said.

She snickered and let out a low mean laugh. And then she hung up.

I turned to Alice who had taken off her dress and panties and bra and lay expectant on the couch. I made some rapid calculations. Five minutes from George's place to the subway, three minute wait, fifteen minute ride, six minutes walk to here, that gave me twenty-nine minutes. I looked at Alice's body and remembered where we had left off. Perhaps I could give it twenty minutes.

It was Swiss. I had to take the entire sexual act and miniaturise it, leaving nothing out, rushing nothing, making it perfect but reducing the scale. I don't know what baroque compulsion required me to squeeze in a perfect mini-fuck before Armageddon descended in the guise of a mad black girl. The most tantalising part was that I refused to look at the clock; it all had to happen using my internal time sense.

Seven minutes, first vaginal caresses; eight and a half minutes, lick clitoris with tongue; twelve minutes, penetration; fifteen minutes, accomplish six variations from behind; seventeen and a half minutes, on her back, knees over elbows, hands on breasts, mouth to mouth, lower angle of entry end penetrate to deepest upper point; now, two and half minutes to ride, wider, wilder, heavier, more sensitive, she responds, she moans, she cries out, the vegatitive tremors begin in my spine; nineteen and a half minutes, and throw open all the switches, pump pump fuck fuck whee whistle bang bang whoosh, and come. Huff huff.

Come on. Get dressed. She is bewildered. I'll explain in the cab. Whirlwind of motion. Confusion. No time for that, just put your underwear in your purse. No time for makeup. Come on. Twenty-six minutes. We are at the door, we are at the elevator, we stand in expectant silence the whole slow ride down. The metal doors open. I step into the lobby.

She is THERE.

130

She stood five foot three, her frizzled hair a huge tangled crown above her head. She wore a brown corduroy jacket and dungarees, no shoes. The jacket sleeves were drenched with blood from each elbow to each wrist, and blood dripped down her fingers onto the fake marble of the lobby floor. She was swaying; her eyes told a story I couldn't bear to read. She peered up out of her daze, looked at me, and some strange focus snapped into place. She recognised me! And then she smiled.

'God,' I thought, 'don't smile. Please don't smile.'

She came up to me. 'Hallo,' she said, and then brushed past, pulled a fiteen-inch butcher knife out of her jacket and went towards Alice. 'First I'm gonna kill that bitch,' she said.

I grabbed her arm; she put the knife in her other hand. My hand went to her wrist; she tried to stab me. She was surprisingly strong. We wrestled for the knife, dancing in the lobby, down the stairs, and into the street. There was no one on the street. A third of the way up East Eighty-second Street, twisting, pushing, cursing. Finally I tripped her, and when she fell, I landed at her side, now pushing the knife back, trying to hurt her wrists so she would drop it. And then I had the flash. A police car turning the corner. Headlights pick up the sight. White man leaning over struggling bleeding black girl wielding huge knife. Bullets fly. Curtains.

'Hey,' I whispered to Beverly, 'if the cops come we're both fucked.'

Her eyes widened. Street wisdom returned. 'Cops?' she said. 'Give me the knife,' I said. I threw the thing down a sewer grate, and helped Beverly back to the building. Suddenly she was a little girl, hurt and aimless. She began to cry. 'Alice, help,' I said.

The beautiful girl came down into the street and put her arms around Beverly's shoulders and held her while I went to the corner to call a cab. The driver was a Jewish grandfather who had probably been in the concentration camps. When we stopped to pick up the two girls, he blinked once. When he turned and asked where we were going, he saw Beverly and gulped. We drove in silence down the East Side Drive on our way to Brooklyn Heights.

He half turned his head. 'Shouldn't we take her to a hospital?' he said.

'Nah, she's all right,' I said. He swallowed again. The tension mounted. He was torn between wanting to keep his cool, to not antagonise the crazies in his back seat, and an overpowering curiosity. Finally, he couldn't hold it in any longer. 'What happened?' he said.

My mind went blank. What kind of story could I make up to cover this?

And from nowhere came Beverly's calm gentle voice. 'We were having a birthday party,' she said, 'and when I went to cut the cake, the knife slipped.'

She leaned back, quite happy with herself. The rest of us rode all the way back with stunned glazed cuckoo clocks ringing in our brains.

Back in Brooklyn, Beverly reverted to type. She jumped out of the cab, and ran to one of the cars that cruise the hookers up and down Atlantic Avenue. She got in, and I could see the man's silhouette as they talked in the front seat. I could imagine what was happening in his head, the struggle between the fear of getting involved with a crazy girl, and the excitement of just what kind of a night he could have with her. In a few moments, the car drove off.

'Well, I don't know what to do,' I had said to Lucinda as she got on the ferry. 'And who can help? Can I go to a therapist? What can I say? "See here, there's a foetus growing in a woman's belly, and I put it there; that is, it is a child that I helped conceive. And I don't want to involve myself in the hassle of seeing it born and raised. Do I have the right to kill it?" What could they say? Yes? No? I think so? And then come up with a list of

132

rationalisations as to why that particular decision was correct?'

She got on the boat. I watched it chug away. 'The baby is in her belly right now, swimming in the amniotic fluid,' I thought. 'To the still dull glow of his consciousness, life is a series of vague movements and sounds, a continual slow growth, a warm cozy ride. He is scheduled, in a little over five months, to come screaming and crashing out of that nest into this most brutal and vicious world, a planetary horror house of human evil. And he will look to two people as the central guides and supports as he matures and learns to make his own way around the contours of the scene. And each of those people he relies on will have been so wasted by the process of civilisation that they can barely, from day to day, manage any form of consistent value, or pattern of ennobling behaviour.

'Your mother is a loser, kid, and your father is a pervert. Your species is suicidal, and the first breath of air you breathe will be polluted, the first drink of water, impure. You will be born under the canopy of restless nuclear bombers prowling the skies, and in the shadow of great phallic missiles. Your birthdate will coincide with the beginning of the rape of Alaska and the destruction of the Amazon. You will grow up in a period of mass starvation. And before you reach maturity, you may be presented with the final spectacle, the end of life on earth. Hoorah, for on the year you were born, we dumped tons of poison gas into the sea. Hoorah, for in the decade you were born, genocide was data-processed for computers.

'With this legacy you can sink to great depths, perhaps write the *Comedy* of our time, Aquarius child who has all the odds against ever seeing the light of day.'

X

What I need, no woman can give. What I want, no man can understand. And yet it seems so simple. It lies in that wordless place, that silent place, that place where everything is small and fragile and clear. I remember moments as a child, when quiet miracles happened, and I gulped and said nothing, because to talk about them was to revoke them, to make them jangling and loud, like the feet of the people who stepped on caterpillars and didn't even notice. Perhaps I seek to return to that crystalline oneness of a child, the hidden joy of a madman.

Or is it merely that the species has passed some point of ecological balance, and it is now dying, and one of its manifestations is my inability to say yes to the child of my loins? The mammals have been in decline for five million years, the naturalists say. No wonder I'm depressed. Perhaps the urge to procreate is atrophied among those of us most sensitive to the vibrations of doom. For me, now, 'us' is always ad hoc. There is no sense of biological loyalty to my murderous kind. The question has become: Who's ready to play, how fast, how high for what stakes?

Degeneracy is the only freedom fascism allows.

It is as though masturbation has become the highest form of sexual gratification. But in these sophisticated times, one generally uses three-dimensional humans to play out the several aspects of the private fantasy. It is a mixed bag. From most people, non-interference is the most I can expect, with some, I am grateful if they play their parts with flair; and rarely, someone comes along who can improvise and teach me something about the workings of my own movie. I imagine that could be considered decadent.

But when my cock is the button and her cunt is the finger pressing it, I ride such a thin line between the grotesque and the sublime that it takes my breath away and I forget to come. For, after all, to come is to beget, and if one will not or cannot beget, there is no point in coming. Without the result of the child, sex is an exercise, a charade, a yoga, a drama, a model for the full panoply of human relations. It is only an art.

In expression, there comes temporary relief from knowing, but it is bought at the price of imposing that knowledge on others. When we fuck, we are always master and slave interchanged, guru and traveller, teacher and student. And if we are going to destroy ourselves and are sickened by the mere thought of bringing children into this world, then let's forget all the Casablanca Bogart you-and-me-forever-baby bullshit. I dig you because you're you, but I dig her because she's her. Just because you're unique doesn't make you special. That goes for me too.

So let's get it on, if we are going to do it, and stop diddling in our pants and private boudoirs and all the icky sniffly little domestic fucks which raise such a loud simper over the whole patriarchal world.

Listen darling, you and I know, or ought to know, that getting fucked controls ever so much more space than the act of fucking. The man is a tool, his cock is a hoe, to be used for weeding and planting. And sometimes his

138

conversation can be amusing. But when he is not performing his proper duty as stud, let him go chase butterflies or tell loud stories about the big buffalo he killed, darling child, while you and I, mother, crawl deeper into the crevices of our violet velour and murmur the real understandings to one another, the sounds that can only be made once, the touches that are symbolic only of themselves.

Suffocating from loneliness, I continued. Back to the house, where the human beings seemed to begin their day. They spoke, they smiled, they enacted the rituals of food. I attempted to peer into the subtleties of their behaviour, to pry into the radiating centres of their astral minds. But I stared at lead walls. All I could receive was the surface. At another time I might be comforted by that superficiality, absorbing it as a welcome change from my own gothic swings from inside to outside. But that day I was embittered.

Francis and Bertha were bickering. There was no subject, no definable point of contention, simply a tension chatter, blowing off the vibrational tangles which had accumulated during the night. In the same way that forest monkeys pick lice from one another's fur, they were engaged in an astral grooming; but not knowledgeable enough to comb auras, they bantered words, as though they could help one another through friction.

Their basic contention was classic: 'He wants her when he wants her, and would prefer that she lose herself the rest of the time, but is willing to play girlfriend games with her to placate her mood. She wants his *time*, the kind of time he uses when painting or doing heavy rapping, and he seems willing to give her that only when he wants to fuck. The rest of each day finds him oddly preoccupied. They have a potentially good trade: she gives pussy, food, continuity, and momma's tit when he needs it; he gives his nerve endings, via his cock or mouth or eyes or mind.

But they have not the slightest hint that they are doing business. She is in the toils of the myth of relationship, and he conspires to support that lie; it is his security as well as hers.'

It was most difficult to probe into the structure of the life they had with each other and light up the basic weaknesses without doing damage to their optimism. But my objectivity ended where my erection began.

'Would you rather die in the arms of the woman you love or in the expansion of your most cherished thoughts?' I asked Francis.

He shot a glance at Bertha.

'You can plead the psychic Fifth,' I said.

He winced at the sarcasm in my voice. With the woman there he would have to fight with one arm tied behind him. But that fact was exactly what I wanted to attack.

Bertha sat at the other end of the round table, drawing obscure multicoloured patterns with a felt-tip pen. Her mouth tightened around a wide smile. 'I'll let that one pass,' he said. 'Your point.'

'Well, then, what's the point?' I countered. 'You're a paradigm maven. I offer you a superior model, or at least demonstrate the obsolescence of your current one, and we can sit and rap about it for hours, but when bedtime comes you take the chick upstairs and I pile into bed alone.'

'Where's Lucinda?' Bertha asked, not raising her eyes.

'I hope she's in the city getting fucked,' I said. 'She was beginning to act as though I were the only man in the world. And you know how much of a drag that can be, don't you dear?'

Francis lit a small cigar. 'I'm not bored with monogamy,' he said.

I refrained from adding, 'So long as you have your women on the side, the ones you never mention to Emily Trueheart here.'

He picked the thought from my brain. 'I've made that

140

scene, I've had as many as three women at once.'

Bertha looked up sharply. 'Where was that? Who were they?' she said rapidly.

'Don't tell her,' I said. 'She'll use it against you.'

'Tell me,' she said.

He hesitated, uncertain. 'It was at Antioch, and it lasted for eight days. It was all I could do to keep the three of them in equilibrium.'

'Was one of them special?' Bertha asked.

Francis looked like a cat with a firecracker up its arse. 'Yeah . . . well, there was Amy, and then she had two friends. I've mentioned Amy to you,' he said to her.

'You didn't tell me *this*,' she said.

'Well,' I purred, 'look how you react.'

She hated me for a brief second and then turned to Francis. 'Amy's in Mexico now, isn't she?'

'I haven't heard from her for a few months,' he said. 'I think she's living with some cat down there.' Bertha relaxed, and returned to her drawing.

'Three at once?' I said. 'What was that like? I've been with three, but only when there were other men. I've never had more than two to myself.'

'Well,' he said, 'I'll have to tell you about it sometime.'

'Why don't the two of you go down to the locker room or something?' Bertha shot up at us.

I whirled towards her. 'Look, my friend and I are continuing a conversation that's been going on for eight or nine years. Now, you've been on the scene a few months. Where the fuck do you think you get the right to act as a roadblock in the work that he and I do together? This kind of conversation only gets salacious when you inject your sniping jealousy. Now you can take him upstairs and gobble him with your greedy little snatch any time you want. I'm not going to give you any substance by pretending to be your rival. I only get naked among friends.'

141

Francis looked out the window.

'All right,' I said to him, 'I'll see you later, or maybe I won't.'

Bertha got frightened. 'Wait,' she said, 'I don't mean you should stop being friends. I just can't compete with the energy you two generate. I just cook and sit in the corner. I don't get to talk. You're too strong for me. I feel left out.'

'Oh baby, don't bring tears to my eyes. What do you want? You won't allow me into that sticky small circle you've drawn around you and him; you disqualify an entire range of communication that can happen between us; you won't fuck me; you won't let him come out with me to go hunting for other women; you have set up a totally inhibitory life style; and now you complain that I am seducing your man away from you.'

She began to squirm. I had her pinned. But I didn't have anything to do with her. I knew what she was suffering, and I was willing to confirm her experience verbally, but I would not bend over backwards to help her out of her plight.

I bracketed both of them with my gaze, helping to cover her nakedness. 'The two of you are as yet unwilling to come to terms with the passion which takes place between men. And you, Bertha, will not let yourself be physically loved by women. You exclude one another from intimate contact with the rest of the human race. My God, that's unnatural, that's a perversion of such magnitude that only in an utterly depraved civilisation such as our own could it not only go unnoticed but be considered the norm.'

Francis nodded and said glumly, 'Polymorphus perverse. I've read Brown too.'

'Reading means nothing!' I was shouting. 'You must live the ideas if they are to mean anything. The point of being familiar with all the life styles is being able to choose which one suits, change modes of living as easily as

142

mathematicians change models.

'But you' – I turned to Bertha – 'won't allow it. You keep him shackled to the prim variations on your tiny theme. I know where that's at. I've been fucked fifty times more often than you have, and by five hundred more different men. I've fucked thousands of women. I know what you dig and how you dig it. There isn't a secret in your cunt, or in your entire body, that I don't know. There isn't an emotion I am not familiar with. You can't make a sound, or an expression, or a movement, that I haven't become a connoisseur of.'

She stared at me hard. 'That's so cold,' she said. 'You completely leave out love.'

'With a purpose,' I thundered. 'Do you dare use that word to describe what goes on between you and Francis? If there were love in you I would sit quietly at your feet. But you are as ruthless and cunning as I am. The only difference between us, baby, is that you play for small stakes, unwilling to gamble past the attainment of your dull linear orgasms.'

I turned to Francis. 'She's right about one thing. You have to choose between us. I won't stop being your friend, and I'll know you a long time after she has become number fourteen on your list of ex-old ladies. But as for now, she wants primary hooks into your being. If I am with you, I will continue to be as eloquent as I can in living and describing my way of life, with all its shit and grandeur. And which runs absolutely antithetical to what she wants! Even if you are swayed only in your head, that will be enough to make her uncertain and fearful. And she is right on in demanding that you don't treat her in such a way as to make her live in fright. So I will step back and respect the walls of formality which must come between us.'

'Don't make me the villain,' she cried.

'Listen, if you won't play with me, and one and one and one isn't three, then the chill is on the lettuce leaf. And

143

it's too bad, because it will be a resentment that will fester inside of him, whether he knows it or not, and just that will pop up at the crucial time in deciding, at some future date, whether you two still have a relationship or not. And maybe now you wish you'd never laid eyes on me.'

She leaned forward in the chair. 'I resent your male chauvinism and your insensitivity towards women.'

I almost hit her. 'Who's been breaking his balls for the last four days to insure that all three voices be heard in this scene? Who has tried again and again to dissolve the false conditioned roles and bring you forth as a person in her own right? And haven't you consistently retreated behind your image as "his woman"?'

She nodded.

'My feelings towards you are the same as towards all other women: benevolent non-recognition. I need cunt, I need tit, I need food. That's woman. The rest is chitchat. I don't know enough about women to form an attitude. As far as I am concerned, men and women are different species. I don't put you up or down. My entire life is just an attempt to understand. Do you understand?'

Francis lit another little cigar. 'He's Valerie Solanas in drag.'

I tried to make sure she was really listening to this. 'It's like men and women are on different sides of a wall. And whenever I need one of the things a woman can give, I go to the wall and negotiate. I presume they do the same from their side. Whatever else you do on that other side of the wall is a mystery to me. Sometimes I put on woman's eyes and take a walk in your world, and I faint from the richness of it. It's gotten to the point where I prefer spending my time there more often. It's such a relief from the cardboard theatrics that men indulge in.

'Look, we fuck or we're alone. When I need to be alone, I go off by myself. When I want other people, then I want to fuck. You understand? That includes touching and

144

talking and sharing vibrations. But serious, and deep. It's strange how you women don't take sex seriously, and yet pretend to yourselves that it is terribly meaningful, whereas men treat it so lightly, but to them it is horribly necessary.'

'You don't think I'm a person,' she said. 'To you I'm just a cunt.'

'Jesus Christ, your cunt is what makes you a woman. Don't you even know that yet? Cunt! Cunt! Cunt!' I yelled, punctuating each word by pounding my fist on the table.

'Not all men think like that,' she said, and simpered at Francis.

'Francis,' I said, 'you been telling this little girl how much you admire her *mind*, man?' He coughed in embarrassment.

'Don't you think I have a mind?'

'Sure you do, and it's a fine mind I'm sure, and you're a good artist, and a good cook, and you have a flair for clothing, and probably reek with marvelous attributes. But that's got nothing to do with the essential reality of the condition that exists between men and women. It's cock and cunt. Do you get that? I don't know how to say it any more simply.' I paused, out of energy for the moment, wondering whether this was all futile. 'Look, there's an easy way to find out just what I'm talking about. Have you ever made it with a woman?'

'No,' she said, harshly.

'Well, the next time you're with one of your girl friends, and when the two of you are really deeply into your closest rap, kiss her on the mouth and fondle her nipples and then go down on her cunt.'

'I don't want to do that,' she said. 'I'm not a lesbian.'

There was a long silence, and she looked thoughtfully from Francis to me and back again. 'What about you two?' she asked. 'Have you been to bed together?'

I looked down at the floor.

'Then everything you're telling me is a lot of shit, she said.

The courage had gone out of me, and suddenly I didn't want to fight any more. It suddenly became very important to end the war

'There are no villains,' I said. 'There is only action. I attack because I'm unhappy, that's all. I don't know how to solve it any more than you do. But please, let's stop pretending that there's no problem.'

'What do you want from me?' she said.

I felt the two of them as a unit, and flashed on my entire relationship with my father and mother. 'I'm not even past the borders of my childhood yet,' I said. 'All I have is my awareness.'

A sweet glow suffused the space and I saw the three of us naked and laughing, rolling in high grass, holding and stroking each other, embracing with trembling sexuality. And a jet plane screeched overhead, shattering the web of possibility. There was no way to sidestep the actual, and the actual was brimming with failure.

Francis looked at me. A shadow of pain crossed his eyes, and then he snapped to, stepping once more into his brisk cheerfulness. 'It's better just to leave it all alone,' he said.

I looked at Bertha. For the first time I could see her helplessness, her fear. And there was no support, no succour for her from the men in her life. She was learning what it meant to be a woman, yet still had much of the little girl in her. Delicious, to be fucking a chick like that. I got a quick insight on what their sex scene was. She would be physically exciting for six months, I imagined. Francis saw me evaluating her. He smiled. 'It's really choice,' he said.

'What does that mean?' she said.

I stood up. 'Sometimes, meaning is a woman,' I said.

I went into the bedroom, smoked a joint, and let my head settle. I heard the two of them go for bicycle rides, return, go upstairs, shower, and clomp into the bedroom. Within ten minutes I heard the bed move, and then the sounds of moans, his excitement and her ecstasy. I yawned. It was all so boring from the outside. But I sent them an abstract blessing, in empathy with their state. Finally, he came. I don't think she did, or if she did, it was a quiet orgasm.

I rolled over and faced the wall. There were the lines I had scrawled while very stoned a few nights earlier:

Sniper sniper sighting tight
In the cosmos of your night
What pope could hold that voidedged heart?
What power dare make it start?

I lay back and let my solitude enter me like a lover, and then I slept.

XI

On the day after Labour Day, Fire Island empties out with the suddenness of a douche bag whose stopper has just been pulled. The slightly shambled secretaries and yellow-rimmed executives finish their summer fuck feast, and go home with memories of near-rapture to sustain them for another brutal New York winter, until the spring arrives again, and the girls don whatever thin things the style moguls have decreed they shall wear that year, and bring to life the great American middle-class crotch once more.

Lucinda had not yet returned from the city. We were on the phone to one another several times each day, the geographic distance between us making possible a regeneration of tender feeling. When I woke up I called her again, but now there was no answer, she had probably gone to a movie. Francis and Bertha were probably still upstairs, sleeping off the aftertaste of their earlier climax. I decided to go for a bicycle ride.

Gliding down the dark paths of the island, a blanket over my shoulders, I threw shadows like a low-flying vampire. Only here and there did lights show in the houses off the walks. It was possible to hallucinate inward images of a thousand historical periods. I was struck by the atemporality of the space, and realised again that the present moment, the now, had no context within which it could be understood. But I was equipped with a spectrum of moods through which to perceive it. It was as though eternity came in flavours, like ice cream. By the time I rolled up to Carol's house, I vibrated in a state of phenomenological flux, and was giddy with the open potential of the moment.

There had been no conscious plan to go there. She lived with her three-year-old son, a lithe and indolent boy; a painter with great personal warmth and mediocre talent; and her mother, a *soi-disant* patroness of the arts who, sadly, had neither the style nor the wit to match her wealth. Visiting that scene was always a mixed bag, but I was hungry for any kind of human contact which involved a familiar face. But when I rode up the inclined path and onto the front porch, I saw no lights. I went around to the back, which jutted out into the bay, and sat on the wide deck, and watched the boats send their mysterious signal lights across the dark water.

The night was heavy with expectancy, the sky a portentous slate grey which showed neither moon nor stars. The only sound rose up from the gentle lapping of small waves against the pier wall which buttressed the property. I felt an odd stirring in my groin. There was something of the secret and hidden about the evening, a sense of murky pleasures about to be unearthed.

I heard a small noise and my skin tingled. I tried to pinpoint the directional source, and found that a very dim light was seeping out from under the door of the small house behind the main building. It was the place where Carol slept with the boy. Ordinarily, given the hour, I would have been to concerned about the impropriety of intrusion to go in there, but a sense of boldness had gripped me. I felt quite reckless.

Inside, lying on a mattress on the floor, was Carol. She wore a flannel housecoat and her eyes were glued to a television screen. I began to tremble. No thought formed in my mind, only a kind of aggressive premonition. I stood there for a full minute, watching the almost imperceptible movements of her body under the cloth, tuning in on her breathing, her tensions. Then she turned around suddenly and saw me.

She went through three changes within a second. At first she was frightened, startled; then she recognised my face and relaxed; finally, sensing my mood, she became fearful again.

I walked to her and stood over her. 'Hello Carol,' I said.

She rolled over onto her back and lay there, looking at me. The space between us congealed and we were locked together in the encapsulating contour of our gaze. I looked at her body very deliberately, as she continued looking at my eyes. Her nipples made mounds under the soft fabric, and the gown caught between her thighs, outlining the bulge of her pubic bone. I could conjure up no picture for arousal. The mere presence of that soft machine had my cock stirring. She looked down and saw the erection beginning. 'Please,' she said, 'just go.' Her tone was that of a dignified housewife to an impudent milkman. She had no way of knowing that I was the White Rabbit with a new taste for leather games.

I stepped onto the mattress.

'You have a strange sense of humour,' she said, trying to make her tone conversational, perhaps thinking to placate me. Oddly, as she responded to my behaviour, my behaviour became more real. There must have been some way for her to refuse to cooperate in such a way as to skewer my role. But, in some confusing way, she was adding fuel to the encounter.

I took my shirt off slowly, my eyes never leaving hers. 'Take that thing off,' I said.

153

The scene took on all the surreal sharpness of a Van Gogh landscape. All the objects in the room stood out in the clarity of form and colour, but ringed with a shimmering aura. Our words and actions fell into slow motion.

I opened my pants and let them drop. My cock was only half hard, and when she saw it, her mouth dropped open. She stared hypnotically. 'No,' she said. Then she shook herself and said. 'No' again, this time simply, matter-of-factly.

I knew there was a bridge I had to cross, and it involved not allowing myself to become embarrassed at the dramatics of the scenario.

It was too late to wonder how I got there, or what her inner drama was. She started to get up. 'This is ridiculous,' she said.

Her words snapped me back to the business at hand. I could almost hear the voice of a director urging me to be more attentive to cues. I wondered what celestial audience this performance was for.

I bent forward and slapped her across the cheek. She fell back. I knelt beside her so I could look into her eyes. I saw a total absence of will. She lay in complete suspension, waiting. Her passivity pleased me, but the impersonality of her mood chilled me. I wanted *her*, not just her body.

For a long moment we remained like that. 'What's your sign?' I said.

She giggled. Carefully, I grabbed the top of her dressing gown and pulled down, ripping it along one seam. I partially lifted her body from the mattress with the effort, and as the lower portion of the gown tore, her naked body fell back. I liked that, the way her body fell.

She lay in the classic pose of pre-ravishment, and I admired the sprawl of her arms and legs, the lay of her breasts, the aroma from her cunt. There was nothing to do now but fuck her.

For the first time I became aware of another presence. The television screen threw its flickering grey shadows over her face, voices floated out of the box. I found myself turning towards it involuntarily as usual.

'This is insane,' I thought. 'We can't stop to look at television.' Carol wasn't moving. I assumed she has resigned herself to the experience and was just waiting for me to get it together.

'When will I see you again? Will I ever see you again?' A man was lowering himself through a trapdoor and looking up into the face of a young woman. She was close to tears.

'I'll come back, after the war,' he said

She seemed taken by a peristaltic spasm, and pressed a rosary into his hands. 'Here, take this,' she said.

'The girl's a nun,' Carol said. 'She's helping him escape from the Germans.'

Her words returned a dangerous quality of surface normality to the scene. I clenched my fists. 'What's the matter?' she said.

'Quickly,' the nun said, 'follow the tunnel until you come to the iron ladder. There will be friends waiting at the top.'

'You don't want me,' Carol said, 'you want my cunt. Why are you wasting your time with me?'

I looked at the tuft of hair between her legs. It seemed utterly trivial. Even in square or cubic inches, it assumed a tiny percentage of the body's total area or volume. It was, literally, a hole. That is to say, an emptiness. And was all this torment over a nothingness?

The man attempted to kiss the nun, but she pulled back, and suddenly he was ashamed of himself. His concept of what a moment of unbearable agony might look like on the face of an American pilot shot down in France during the war was etched by a billion electrons against a curved sheet of coated glass. 'God bless you,' the nun said.

I sank to my knees and then lay full-length on the mattress. Carol rolled to one side.

Suddenly the door burst open and four Nazi soldiers spilled into the room. One was a colonel and the others were enlisted men. The colonel grabbed the nun by the wrist and twisted her arm, but by this time she had closed the trapdoor and covered it with the rug. 'Where is he?' he said. He spoke with a German accent. 'If you don't tell us, I will turn you over to my men, and they will not only torture you, but . . . ' He let the silence trail off and raked her body with his eyes glowing like dislocated diamonds.

Her face showed the expression which the actress probably considered went with the feeling, *A fate worse than death*, and she broke free and ran out of the room.

Three submachine guns rattled into the darkness. The screen cut sharply to the front yard of the house. The girl was lying on her back. Oddly, her face held the kind of beatific smile one would expect of a nun who has just been martyred to save her virginity, an American bomber pilot, and the matchlessness of five distinct myths. The colonel's face softened. 'She was too pure for this world,' he said, turning on his heel, and strode away. The final shot was of the nun's face surrounded by a four-inch aura. The screen went dark and obscure music played.

I knelt between Carol's legs, rubbing the outer lips of her cunt with the thumb of my left hand, and nudging my cock along the inside of her right thigh. I felt no passion, no excitement, no interest. I grabbed my cock with my right hand and brought it to the cunt lips I had now partially parted. She ground her pelvis gently up and forward, inviting me to enter her. 'Fuck me good,' she said, 'I haven't been fucked good in a really long time.'

For the next half hour I fucked her with the concentration and *sang froid* of a masseur. I took a certain chilly technical pride in the accomplishment. With no real difficulty I opened the layer after layer of resistance, lodging finally into the deepest possible cunt of her cunt. She had countless orgasms, great shuddering affairs which bunched the muscles in her belly, and made her emit a noise like a vigorous death rattle. When I had completed the entire set of postures, the exercise was completed, and like a Tai Chi practitioner who comes to the end of the series, I simply came to rest. After a while my erection subsided, and I sat back.

'You didn't come?' she asked with some surprise after she had pulled herself together. I abstractly admired the sheen of sweat on her skin, the hardness of her nipples, the utter abandon of the angle of her legs and the cant of her cunt. She shrugged. I changed the channel.

Raquel Welch was saying, 'The mind is the most erogenous zone of all.' David Frost, a slight tic developing near his right eye, said, 'What do you mean by that?' And she knighted him with a look of disdain he richly deserved. Carol started sucking my cock. 'I smoke too much dope,' I thought. 'It interferes with my concentration.'

She fell into the greedy-gobbling-child pose, lying on her side, her knees to her chest, both hands around my cock, pulling it into her slackly open mouth. The pressure on the base, the friction against her lips, and the sweet sensation of her wet tongue hitting the tip each time she pulled, quieted my thoughts. She was most gentle and loving, lapping, juice-hungry. I could have come easy, but I changed my ways.

I sat on her chest and lifted her head from behind, bringing her mouth up. I slipped a pillow under her head, freeing my hands. Then I fucked her in the mouth, penetrating her throat until she gagged, then pulling out and letting her splutter around the tip of my cock, whimpering and licking, finally taking the meat into her mouth again. That was quite exciting and I shot a very heavy deposit of swirled sperm onto her tongue, and she

157

swallowed until my entire cock was drained, and then kept her mouth on me until I had grown totally limp.

'Would you like some coffee?' she said.

'Would you like to stay the night?' she said.

'Would you like to fuck me again?' she said.

And added, 'Any way you like.'

During the night I woke and heard her mumbling and moaning in her dreams. I wondered what sort of interior life she had, and speculated on how tedious it might be getting to know her. I glimpsed an impulse to wake her up, to talk to her, to ask directions to the person. But all the experience of my life brayed with laughter, and I closed my eyes to wait for sleep again.

In the morning I dressed before she woke up. 'You're going?' she said as I went. 'The others won't be back until tomorrow.'

'It's better that I leave,' I said, cursing myself for the quality of dialogue, blaming it on the television.

XII

The price for pleasure is certainty. Perhaps that is too flip. Pleasure underscores the reality of dying, for the same process of letting go takes place in both manifestations. But of course, the French refer to orgasm as the little death, and the Tibetans picture their Tantric deity with a string of skulls hanging from his scrotum.

My life is plagued by a conditioned search for the ultimate. My mind has been made hierarchical by the frocked fiends who seized me when I was totally vulnerable to impressions and fed me with winged strictures. The journey has been an odd one, although reducible to statistical normalities, and has led me into the arms of women who wondered at my desperation. Understanding that no final solace lay in any woman's arms was the most difficult disillusionment.

Prior to that I went the conventional route, first seeing the priests and politicians as playing the most ancient and sweeping of con games, pretending to represent a power greater than themselves. But so many of them are ugly in their eyes and mouths that a direct glance is enough to unmask their rhetoric and perceive them as hollow and vicious tricksters.

More subtly, I yearned towards the abstract as the end of my quest. I phased through the appreciation of pure thought, or truth, or beauty, or Absolute Reality, as the ideal. It took a while to learn that I was merely kneeling before the rationalisations of my own projections.

Finally, I fell into the swamp of experience. If, I concluded, I experienced the fact of existence for myself, if I knew terror and joy and bliss and boredom for myself, through experience, then I would know all that it is possible for a person to know. Naively, I neglected to come to terms with the 'I' who was experiencing. When 'I' knew something, I had to ask myself, 'Which "I" is this?'

At which point I cursed the Pope and all his legions, and surrendered to a state of vacuous vibration, disdaining all the products of my mind as so much read-out having to do with nothing except the internal state of the think machine. Practically every value held by the moiling majority of my species, I have discarded as worthless, only to rediscover the organic immediate basis upon which the phony historical morality is based. I have let all this learning be fired with a river of LSD, and become transmogrified. I am now a mutant. The soft machine is still the same as all the others which walk around and practise the dances of their days, but the person inside has become alien, essentially *other* than those who gave him birth.

'Daddy, why is the grass green?'

'*Why* is an inadmissible question except as used by Heidegger in "Why are there essents rather than nothing at all?" If you wish to understand the *how* of grass and green, look to science.'

The son of the mutant grows up.

Now the summer vacation was over, and it was time to centre ourselves once again in the city, amidst the decay, the poisoned sky. Lucinda had gone in earlier to take care of business and now three of us sat on the train, Francis and Bertha in glum hostility. The air conditioning in our car didn't work, and we were too steeped in the undulating frisson of masochism to change cars.

I went for some water and met Patricia, the dark and moulded airline stewardess I had met on the Island. We rapped for a while. We flirted with our eyes. I went with her back to her seat and for a few minutes we shared the view of auto graveyard and sooty lumber factories which line the route of the Long Island Railroad.

We traded body cues across the space between the seats, and at one point she slipped her hands between her legs and bounced her thighs from side to side. I took a number of quick polaroid shots of her, the delicacy of her upper lip dewdropping forward at the center, the dark spaces under her blouse which show the size of the aureola around each nipple, the curve of one cheek bulging out where she sits. I noted the long fingers, and the suppleness of her waist as she twisted around and bent slightly to one side. She was an exquisite morsel, her flesh alive, and she being chatty, intelligent, and familiar with the major cities of the world.

I fantasised spending an evening with her, but within a flash comprehended the totality of the night. I realised that there would not be one unrehearsed word, not a movement which sang with spontaneous passion. We were both very hip, chic, sophisticated, jaded. We understood the intricacies of pseudo-intimacy perfectly. I would be thrilled at discovering the texture and smell and sound of her, but I would not be surprised. I was almost stunned by my own ruminations. In an instant I had reduced her to an old movie, pleasant enough to see again, but only if one had nothing else to do.

And what else was there to do? I suddenly seemed to be staring down a long narrowing tunnel which had a brick wall at its end. I looked down the abstract contour of my

163

own life and found it empty. And the only thing to relieve that emptiness would be the conflict I might find in engaging myself in some project with another, in some war. I had come to the end of my tether, and even the prospect of twelve hours of fresh, never-before-tasted, hot and dripping cunt left me uninterested.

'Then how will I amuse myself?' I thought. And then, 'What a shallow epicure I have become.'

I sighed and found myself looking into Patricia's eyes. She smiled coolly, as though she were reading my thoughts. I lit a *Gitanes*. We became very suave for a while, sharing our effete mutual self-consciousness.

'One can always take refuge in boredom,' I said. 'If we had a closed car, you would kneel before me and take my limp warm penis in your mouth, and lap at it gently until it became firm, and then nibble until it was hard, and then suck until I sprayed your mouth with sperm. And all the while I should continue to smoke, and gaze out the window, gently contemplating the destruction of a civilisation, the end of the culture, the curtains on history.'

Her breathing became ever so slightly more quick and her lips glistened. She looked quickly around the car without moving her eyes. I saw the non-movement and flashed that she was looking for some safe spot where we could go for the few minutes necessary.

'Yes,' I said, 'our grey convoluted lives sparked only by the most tawdry petty spectacles. If I had you alone I would insert my entire clenched fist into your cunt and punish you with my wrist.'

Her jaw went slack. She was already on the edge of a mild hypnotic stupor. I stood up abruptly. 'Forget everything I have said,' I said.

Francis looked up from his bout of hatred with Bertha. They were in the ninth round of a scheduled fifteen-rounder. 'If I were a shallow and utterly worthless hedonist,' I said, 'against what criteria could that be measured?'

'Importance is just a matter of timing,' he said. 'When the connection happens, it's all there. When it doesn't happen, there's nothing you can do about anything. Then it's best to sit down and read a book.'

'What are you talking about?' said Bertha.

XIII

For a few brief weeks in the fall New York is habitable. The hot air masses are sharply cut through one night by a clean chill wind from the North. And for a time the negative ion content increases, and one can almost smell the air which usually serves as nothing but a cushion for the clouds of death which spew from cars and factories. People walk more briskly but are in less of a hurry. And a sense almost of what used to be called humanity pervades the town.

There must be an instinct in our species which tends us towards the destruction of the weak. Before the junk-yard of civilisation was organised to insure that the aged and infirm are at least taken care of, those who could not keep up on the hunt were killed or abandoned. Now, living our lives of concrete cycles, we roar down trails of psychic exploitation, and the hunt has shifted its milieu. Food is brought in by ship and truck and train from farms and slaughterhouses thousands of miles away. And we in the capitol have nothing more crucial to do than maintain the equilibrium of the zombies and cripples who perambulate this great buzzing crypt.

The basic human emotion is terror, which sometimes softens to poignancy. All but the tiniest percentage of our business each day is a millennia-bound routine to mask that state. We keep busy so we have no time to perceive the truth of our cosmic condition. And leaders, the boss monkeys, of any circle, exploit the blindness and fear of the millions, the sleep-walkers, sending them into carnage and bondage, buying them with paper and promises of paradise.

The night after returning to the city, I received an invitation to Jessica's birthday party. She was one of a group that had come together to launch one of the new growth centers which are rapidly replacing revival meetings as America's number one religion. Since they were New Yorkers, however, they had accrued enough layers of cynicism concerning the entire process of cash-on-the-line help-for-your-soul scene to make interesting company. They were fairly unsophisticated game players, and their success in manipulating groups of people came largely from the hunger of their customers to be had. Lucinda was doing battle with nausea from the pregnancy and opted to stay home.

Jessica was twenty-four that night, a tall, flaxen-haired Virgo who had very early tripped over the problem of discerning illusion from reality, and had not yet tired of the guessing game to settle into the final understanding that what *is* subsumes all dualities in an inexorable present tense. Dan and Jean hosted, and provided the context for the evening with the solid vibrations of their two-year marriage. Dan had been heavily into politics and had to come to the conclusion that the only meaningful political statement left was dynamite, and not wanting to take that route, had lapsed into the sensitivity syndrome, and was planning to open a place 'in the country'. John was there, a true innocent from Minnesota all caught up in the complexities of his genius, and his old lady Janet, who

170

could still blow everyone's mind by idly reaching over to John while he was rapping with someone, to take his prick out of his pants, and nonchalantly suck him off. Hal rounded out the company, going on endlessly about the play he was writing which concerned his vision for an encounter Utopia. We smoked parsley flakes sprayed with PCP.

'Everyone's two-dimensional,' I said.

'No, you're projecting,' Jean said.

After that, chaos seized the time.

John put on a reel of eight millimetre pornography, seemingly shot sometime during the 30's. It showed a heavily made-up woman being fucked by two men. They went through the routine with frozen expressions. He swung the projector over to show the film on Janet's belly and thighs.

I faded again, blinking into invisibility, letting the thereness of the others spring into fullness of focus.

'What odd animals they are,' I said to the silence. 'How they bruit about and sweat all over their skins and make noises with their mouths. They live in a perpetual excitement, an inability to lie down except to become unconscious. I see them in their shuffling nakedness, and in the stench of their decomposition.' I jumped up. 'Giddy fucking bacchanalia!' I shouted. 'Overripe and rotten fruit. Sweet decay.' I took my shirt off and staggered into the bedroom. The synthetic cannabis had stunned my body into numbness and no censor guarded my tongue. I fell across the bed and watched myself in the mirror nailed to the ceiling. My body sprawled, not belonging to me, the sensuality of the tripping decadence of drugs and dying city life make my cock tingle with a thousand pinpoints of disgust. The stench of existence exploded in my nostrils. I was ready to be the corpse served, still twitching, to the fat baron.

'I'm trapped in illusion again,' said Jessica as she stalked

171

into the room, her eyes wide with horror. Behind her the ragged laughter of demented people.

'Stop that,' I said.

'I'm at the edge,' she said, and licked her lips. Her cunt poked its way through the air as she walked towards me. The din swamped my mind. All control was lost. The focus of my eyes unscrewed and the impressions flew in unstructured. Her face kept changing. Innocence peaked and crashed into nostrils of a leper. Flawless skin, prodding me, torturing my balance, my precarious equilibrium in the nothingness.

'Where's Lucinda?' she said.

For a moment the words rasped across my eyes in a loathsome ugliness. I snapped back to the surface. It was Jessica, twenty-four years old; this was her birthday party; we had fucked three times over the past year; in the context of consciousness, I knew her. 'Is Lucinda coming?' she said.

The searing guilt of the impending abortion and my inability to feel anything about it except impatience cut at me. I began to sob. I curled inside myself and brought my knees to my chest.

'What's wrong?'

'I don't know, I just came in to talk to him and he started crying.'

'Is he crazy?'

The voices of the people buzzed around and around. I spun more deeply into the sticky blackness of my pit and strained to make sense of the sounds.

'It's almost as though he can hear us,' said Jessica, and then I knew. She was in my head too. She saw, and she kept two levels going. She kept saying the words which had meaning. John sat on the bed. 'Sliding into the slough of despair again, eh?' he said, poking me in the ribs.

Groups splintered, conversations flowed and waned, dope made the circuit once more. I sucked greedily on the pipe, yearning desperately for the solace of madness to take me once more into the torment of certainty. It was a party, a birthday party. Jessica put her right hand on my crotch and began fondling my genitals. Swiftly, gently, she prodded and touched, she drew the concentration of pleasure to the tip. She seduced me from my jagged solitude and while I succumbed I hated her. She licked my nipples, she gave me promises with her lips. Her cunt grew enormous and threatened to swallow my entire body. I braced myself against the entrance to her womb.

She fell face forward and huddled there. 'I want you to come home with me tonight,' she said. 'You have a girl friend staying with you,' I said. She looked hurt.

I raked her face with my fingers and drove them into her mouth. She whimpered and licked at them with her tongue. I bent forward and chewed at her chin and neck, taking painful bites. I ground my knuckles into her nose, smashing it against her face.

'The next time I fuck you I want to hurt you,' I said. 'You know that. Having someone in the room who doesn't understand the game will prevent me. What's the point?'

'The Game,' she whispered, and her face went white. 'Yes,' I hissed into her ear, 'You want to play the Game too. More than anything else. Everything else is shallow, is stupid.'

In one stroke I had regained my autonomy. From deepest madness I sprang instantly to perfect reason. And with that, she capitulated. I grabbed her hard by the cunt, bunching the lips in my fingers. 'Don't hurt me,' she moaned. I twisted. 'Oh, please hurt me,' she whispered.

John and Janet came in. Confusion multiplied. Each of us looking to the others for a clue as to what to do next. We were the shock troops for a bloody orgy, but we had to get ourselves in sync.

'Everybody say what they want,' Janet said. 'I'll start.' She paused. 'I want to fuck,' she said. 'That's all I really

173

ever want to do.'

John nodded. 'I want to sleep and fuck, not necessarily in that order.'

They looked at me. 'I want to crash for the rest of the evening. I don't care where. If you all stay here, I'm going back up to Lucinda's pad. If you go to Jessica's, I'll ride with you.'

'Let's go to my place,' Jessica said.

We made our farewells and went out into the street. I felt as though I were covered with thick cotton gauze. Dan and Hal walked us to the car, since St. Marks Place at two in the morning had the ambience of a crazed speed freak slashing at the air with a razor. We drove to the West Village where the liberals and the homosexuals still kept the peace.

I entered into a state of powerlessness, a wood chip on a stream. I basked in the rare space of active willessness. We piled into the tiny room, Kay, the girl from California staying with Jessica, and in a few moments had the stereo working and more dope passing the periphery of the circle. All the threads of my psyche were becoming unravelled and I just wanted to lie down and pee in my pants. I was stoned on regression.

The sofa was opened into a bed and it took up almost all the available floor space, so the five of us piled onto it. We made some cosmic chitchat and listened to McCartney play *McCartney*. John sat at the edge of the bed, trying to get into Kay's cunt via eye twinklings and flat-palmed touches. I lay back, with Jessica on one side and Janet on the other. I lolled back and forth, from the tall clean girl on my left to the short rapacious witch on my right. I was the ridgepole delineating yin yang.

The three of us got into one another's breathing and body sense, and as we listened to the music that magic moment happened when we all knew we were hearing and responding in exactly the same way. Jessica moved over

174

and lay on her back between my legs, her coccyx pressing into my pubic bone. She and Janet held hands.

When the drum-and-breathing solo came on, I flipped out into a non-verbal awareness and began to wail, flailing my thighs and running my hands over Jessica's body. She pressed herself into me, but stilled my fingers. I let my arms drop and immediately became quiet. With that, she let a series of small shudders go down her spine, and I felt myself closing around her. For an instant it seemed that she was a man lying face down on me, fucking me, and I was responding with the most delicate of pressures. Meanwhile, Janet and I had got into perfect head contact, matching the astral velocities as we skiied downhill at faster and more reckless speeds. The two women welded the triangle shut, and the three of us sailed into a superb dance, with the energy flowing physically between me and Jessica, emotionally between Jessica and Janet, and cerebrally between Janet and me. We rode together to the end of the cut, and rose to a three-way climax that was split-second perfect.

We all let out a sigh at the same time. Janet turned and said, 'Wow, four orgasms in my head.' And Jessica twisted around, moved up, brushed her mouth lightly against mine, and said, 'You are beginning to understand.'

I got up and went to piss. When I returned, Jessica and Janet were sitting cross-legged facing one another, doing a dance with their arms. Kay was nodding out in a rocking chair in the corner, and John was snapping his fingers into the non-operational fireplace. I stood next to him for a moment, and suddenly spasm of aching longing seized my groins.

'So this is what it is like to be a woman,' I thought. I groaned out loud and leaned halfway over. John turned to the girls and said, in a cockney accent, 'Hey, me mate 'ere got a case of 'ard nuts. Now you females 'ave been fussin' and fondlin', but you've left this poor chap all

175

knotted up.Now, oo's gonna take care of him?'

The night lost its boundaries. We were committed to total purgation, but I was the only one in the room who understood that. To them, it was just a flippy night out, an extension of the party, while down my veins whistled the winds which rocked the trees where witches howled at the stars. We were moving, and moving. Through the sky, through the system, through the galaxy, through the universe, through time, through space, through the mocking smile of eternity. And we were always crumbling, always at the edge of extinction, like frantic candles doomed from the moment they are lit.

I stared into the swirl of flesh with eyes that saw too much.

And Jessica slipped inside my mind. For a raging instant of sheer fury I attempted to crush her body with the massive doors which guarded my palace of perception. She answered with the tiniest and most ineffable of questions. I crashed down the gates of pain.

'If you want me, you have to swim the moat,' I said. The others blinked their eyes. I turned to them. 'Intimacy comes from release, not from practice,' I said in explanation.

Janet took John's clothes off. She organised an experience, having all of us slap and caress and rub his body. The sight of his cock inflamed me, and I caught myself from leaning forward and taking it into my mouth. Just that afternoon I had dipped into the Ansonia Baths for a quick steam, and spent a rapturous ten minutes sucking a ponderous eight-inch cock, revelling in the sheer sensuous joy of it, realising that I had ultimately erased all value as to the concavity or convexity of the sexual organ I put in my mouth.

I put on Josh White's *Prison Songs* and we did a number on John's back. But I soon grew bored with the endless titillation to no end.

'Listen darlings, I'm tired of all this Esalen nonsense. Are we going to get to it, or shall I go to sleep?'

Unreal, unreal, reality reeling. I crawled up past Jessica and lay down against the backrest of the couch. She lay on top of me and Janet sprawled out beside John. Very soon, we were all nodding out. I got uncomfortable and went to get a drink of juice. Jessica stirred. 'What do you want?' she said. 'I want to piss, I want to drink, I want to smoke, I want to fuck, I want to sleep,' I said, 'in that order.'

Perhaps it was my act of impatience which short-circuited the festivities. But it didn't matter. Chronological time passed no matter what we did. The abortion of an orgy seemed of no more consequence than the abortion of a baby. Everything which begins must end. So why start anything in the first place? Now that my cock was quiescent, I had no regrets. I went into the john and sat down for a long time. I read *An Illustrated History of Love*, and when I went back into the bedroom, the four of them were asleep. I put two pillows on the floor and stretched out, prepared for a lengthy vigil.

I didn't move. I didn't pull a single string on any plane of consciousness. And I was surprised when Jessica got up and came to lie next to me. Part of me didn't want to touch her. I was exhausted.

For the next half hour she licked my body. I filled up with an old sadness and longing. It had been many years since I had hung so nakedly between need and pride, and this girl-woman next to me was manoeuvring me into the classic position of love's pain, suggesting that we tie ourselves together and go stand at the edge of the cliff. At this point, I could still master the nuances of the game. But I had no confidence in my ability to sustain the tension. I was losing interest in all the pockets of expression left open to the denizens of a dying world.

She moved up until her eyes were on mine. She silently

177

implored me to let her in. But at this moment Lucinda was tossing in her nightmare, while the baby burned in the docket, on trial for his life. And here was the judge wondering whether to despoil another human being. A young, hungry, soft girl who didn't understand how strong her need for destruction was.

And then, with the delicacy of a cloud scudding from in front of the sun, the matter became unimportant. It wasn't me against her, not now, but the two of us caught in a scene written to a scale far beyond our abilities to comprehend. What difference whether I fucked her or not, hurt her or not? When you've destroyed one human being, you've destroyed us all. And it is possible to acquire a taste for the process, growing more subtle, able to play hide-and-seek with one's motivations, pretending to oneself that one is in love again, or simply seeking sex again, while the unrelenting hidden purpose is murder.

She had only her panties on and I was naked. I could feel our complementary vacuums raging inside and between us. We kissed and my mouth clamped onto hers; I sucked the air from her lungs and rolled my tongue deep into her throat. She brought her hands to her chest like a puppy begging for food. Her hair kept swirling between us, getting into our teeth and eyes. I whipped my head back and growled and she rolled face down. I came up next to her and ran my hand over her arse, feeling the thin cotton fabric slide over the mounds of flesh. Neither of us made a sound except for the deep regular breaths which made our heads buzz.

I reached down between her thighs, feeling the irresistable curve of flesh formed by her cheeks, and ran one finger against her cunt from the outside of her panties. The cloth was soaked with her secretions, and I felt my chest melt as I rubbed and prodded deep between her legs, massaging her cunt lips, cupping her entire pubis with my hand. For a very long time we did nothing but concentrate

178

on the joyous waves of fulfilled yearning which flowed from the heat of the inside of her body and the tingling of my fingers.

She came to a climax as I pushed down and caressed her clitoris.

We rested awhile and then she reached down to grab my cock in her hand again. She squeezed it tightly, all the while pushing against my belly with her elbow. It was as though she wanted to rip the thing out by the root. It seemed clear to me that just then she really wanted me to be a woman. But no matter how feminine my soul, there was still the cock to contend with. And we blended at a nebulous moment of decision to get the stiff thing out of the way in the most organic manner possible, to force it to ejaculate.

I slipped her panties down to just below the bottom line of her buttocks. I tugged to get them down further, but she grabbed my wrist. She looked into my eyes, screwing her head around over her shoulder, and flashed me a negative signal. She was saying no!

I suddenly remembered similar scenes many years ago with Connie, when I had wrestled for hours attempting to resolve the yes-no conflict within her. I had been one of the headiest forms of excitement, but it could be countenanced only as long as it was understood as merely another variation of the Game. When it became a sub-game in its own right, it grew tedious.

I waited a moment until she had stopped holding me back, and when she was lying quietly again, I raised my body and lowered onto hers. My limp cock nestled at the base of her arse, and I rocked back and forth until it grew hard, and I could feel her responding. I lifted up and changed the angle of approach until I was between her legs, the head of my cock nudging at the tip of her cunt lips. There was no fever in me at all. Mostly, I didn't want to lose the immense silence which enmeshed us both. More than anything it was important to keep the utmost mutuality, that she know exactly what I was doing in my body and in my head, and that I feel every subtle response and initiative she made. In short, it didn't matter what we did, so long as we hummed together.

I pressed deeply into her and she pushed back against me, her buttocks fitting perfectly into the hollow formed at my groin. When she lifted so high that her thighs left the floor, I slid one hand under her. The feel of her flesh was electric. The top of her panties cut into my balls, stimulating me more than her fingers could have done. I pressed my cock into her from below, not penetrating her, but making the head of it ride down the length of the wet lip and into the clitoris. She twitched and moaned a bit.

'I am consciously doing this and you are consciously doing this and we are riding the edge of ecstasy and communion,' I said into her ear, and then plunged my tongue into that ear, causing her to bunch in the middle.

As I got more heavily into the actuality of our mutuality, she became hotter and wetter until she collapsed in a series of small shudders which marked another climax.

I waited for several breaths and then gently entered her. She flinched, and I froze. That was where she was frightened. I let the pressure of my organ just rest in her until she was comfortable with it, and then relaxed my muscles, letting my weight drive me into her as far as our position would allow. She let out a long sigh. I suddenly fell deeply in love with her.

'Stop that,' I said to myself, but it was too late.

'Jessica,' I said.

She brought her arse up so that my cock would enter her more fully, and then she started to grind against me, bathing me with the full lusciousness of her gift, the access to her body and the openness of her heart. I felt the entire length of her, legs against legs, back against belly. My arms lay at full contact along her side and one hand still cupped

180

her cunt as my cock slid in between my fingers. The utter fragility and purity of the moment melted all my reserves.

She was yielding herself up, sucking at me with her cunt, shooting the heated pleasure into my cock. I rested my forehead on her skull and blended the electricity of my brain with hers. Once again, for the first time, there ceased to be me and her, there was only the act. It seemed as though her body was sobbing with joy.

She brought her pelvis up, back, and down in a circle. Each movement away pulled at all the nerves in my cock, making the blood rush to the sensitive tip. Each movement towards me had me sinking sliding into her, touching the pit of her cunt, sending the current into her belly. At one point between in and out, Lucinda's face bloomed in the darkness, and the entire room rocked on its hinged foundation.

I cried out and then felt the beginning of my orgasm. I changed gears in my consciousness and continued to ride the cresting wave with unflagging awareness. She felt it also, and tuned herself to receiving the substance I was about to have explode from me. This was to be my orgasm, but shared by both of us.

Just before I came, she spread her legs the slightest bit wider, and opened more fully to me. With a long silent yell I let my physiology run its course, and my body bucked into her with all the padded fury of a mammoth ferry slamming into its slip. We strained at the peak until I had released every last spasm, and then she sank to the floor, her cunt contracting wildly and spasmodically.

We drifted off into the state between wakefulness and sleep, into the area of thought-dreams. I felt some slimy force rousing itself in me, and the sickeningly familiar symptoms of withdrawal flared in my belly. A terrible mixture of anxiety and revulsion. I looked at the existential monster sliding up from its foul corner of the soul and caught its full ugliness in my gaze. For a long long time we stood locked in deadly energy combat or struggle. And with a sharpness that brought me to my knees, a blinding flash of yellow light exploded above our heads, and the beast dispersed in its shadow.

Jessica stirred at precisely that instant. 'Oh,' she said, 'you're here. Thank God you're here.'

'I almost slipped off,' I said.

She twisted her body under me so that I now lay in her embrace. We locked gazes and shared the afterbreath of fear, the knowledge of those who have felt the cold touch of the Alien at the moment of perfect intimacy. Her body was solid under mine. We copped out to perfection.

I got up off her, lay by her side, and as she cuddled to my chest, we fell asleep.

XIV

'Well, there are so few things left for you. You might as well attempt being noble.' Lucinda's voice had the edge of a cat's mating yowl. We had been back in the city for a week. I had reached that point of inner desperation where time scratched across my consciousness like fingernails across a blackboard. I was caught in a matrix of selfconscious gestures, aware of the awful imminence of our situation, and incapable of doing anything but accelerating the proprieties.

I had just been invited to another party. John and Janet had dropped acid with several other couples and were now enjoying a mass naked freak-out, up and down the levels of their ground-floor pad, with its murky basement and surprising garden. But Lucinda held me with her need. Outwardly calm, she leaned dangerously into hysteria. I wondered about suicide, but felt no vibrations in that area. Leaving her now would be to turn my back on her pain.

I said no to Janet.

'I understand what you're doing,' she said, and I heard the solid thud of her words chugging out from the welter of acid energy. 'You are my brother,' she said.

Lucinda lay across the bed, her eyes closed, her mouth half open. I saw myself go over to her and simply take my pleasure with her lips and tongue. Technically, she was about the best blow job of any woman I had known, and as good as all but a few men. I found myself thinking, 'If I stay here tonight I not only get a chance to be noble, but I get my cock sucked too.' I wondered whether I was despicable.

I hung up and lit a joint. Lucinda joined me. We got high very quickly, with fine flourishes of rushes in our heads. At the end of empire the rulers are granted grand gestures while the plebs celebrate annihilation with drugs. If this is the last time 'round, it is the time for bitter laughter.

'Francis is henpecked,' I said.

'You lie as much as he does,' she said.

'And I don't like that girl of his. That's all. She just gives me a bad feeling.' I began pacing up and down.

'Francis is just playing the two of you off against each other,' Lucinda said.

I looked at her. 'When the foreplay goes out of a relationship, it's a good bet that the tenderness is gone also. Why aren't you more aggressive? It might have been possible if you were more aggressive.'

'You said you didn't want any problems from me. I'm just here for when you want me. In a woman, aggression is abandon. You ought to know that.'

I sat on her chest. My cock dangled over her face. 'Do you want the baby?' I asked.

She took the limp organ between her teeth and flicked at the tip of it with her tongue. It got hard. She leaned back. 'Yes, I want the baby,' she said.

'Then why don't you have it?'

'I don't want to raise it by myself. I don't want to be left alone in this apartment having to take care of a baby. You aren't going to stay around.'

186

I leaned forward and came to rest on my elbows so that I was crouched over her. I dropped my cock into her waiting mouth, and as she sucked on it I thought about what she had said. But the impossibility of coming to a decision which wasn't a bad one, coupled with the growing sensation at my crotch, soon dispersed all cohesion. I fucked her in the mouth for about ten minutes, pushing into her throat to make her gag and then pulling out, leaving her gasping at the experience of pseudo-terror she had just had. I hit against her lips, knowing they would be bruised for hours afterwards, and each time she smiled or spoke, the throbbing ache at her mouth would trigger this entire scene to mind.

'Beverly used to vomit all over my cock.' I said. 'She would go down so hungrily that she kept gagging until she threw up. And then she would keep sucking until I came into her mouth.'

My words inflamed Lucinda, and she lapped the length of my cock with broad strokes of her tongue. She was beginning to go wild a little.

'There were three women besides yourself who were the best,' I mused out loud. 'Beverly, Wendy, and . . . ' I paused. 'I can't think of her name,' I said. 'And I really dug her. That's sad.' I tried to picture her. 'She was short and she used to teach bellydancing.'

Lucinda stopped abruptly, caught by a thought. 'Did they fuck as good as you do a man?' she asked.

'As good as I do a man? Them, as women?' I was puzzled.

Lucinda got exasperated. 'Oh, do they do it as good as you! That's all.'

I thought about it a while and she snuggled back into my cock. 'They were as passionate, but not as inventive.'

She brought her legs up and hooked them into my elbows. I leaned forward and her cheeks caved in with suction. 'You certainly suck a lot,' I said. 'I mean, as opposed to lick or bite.'

'Is that good?' she said, her mouth still full.

'Anything is good,' I answered, 'so long as it's contrasted with its opposite.' She was bent like a yoga instructor in an esoteric pose. Her cunt winked out from between her buttocks. 'I wish we had another man now,' I said. 'Look at that. An entire erogenous zone going unused.'

'Well, if you can find one within the next few days, bring him around,' she said. 'After the abortion I won't be able to fuck for a month.' She looked as thoughtful as a woman could with a cock nudging her lips. 'I haven't gone that long without fucking for fifteen years.'

'Fuck a lot, do you?' I asked.

'Twenty-five men in the last six months before I met you. But I was tired of fucking men. I do it with you because I'm used to you.'

'If I had my way,' I said, 'I mean, if it were physiologically possible, I would fuck about forty per cent of all the women I see. Worldwide that would make about half a billion women. Assuming that all of them would want to fuck me, but I'm not going to let such a dismaying reality intrude on my fantasy.'

'You bastard,' she said, 'don't let any *reality* intrude on your precious fantasies.'

'That's all words anyway. Here is something else.' I moved back and inserted my cock into her cunt. We began a very odd fuck. It is impossible to describe its rich ambiguities without destroying the memory of its fragile strength in my mind. It's too hard to write about that.

After the dissipation of the seventh wave, the cresting of the sex and emotion that makes for orgasm, I realised that I wasn't going to ejaculate and I simply didn't have the stamina to keep us both reaching for the next climax. I tore loose from the magnetic interlock of cock and cunt and threw myself on my knees at the edge of the bed where her arse now hung half over. My mouth and tongue went immediately to work on her slippery cunt lips, now the texture of well-polished, well-used leather.

As I started to speak that most ancient of languages, the marriage of touch, movement, and poetry, the phone rang. I thought it was Janet and for an instant a picture of the party flashed on my inner eye. I was impelled to answer. On the third ring, I ripped my mouth away from Lucinda's body and stomped to the phone. It was Bertha. I listened as her thin voice informed me that they would not come to the movies with us that evening. I suddenly remembered we had a tentative date. I almost choked with chagrin. I spat out a few words to maintain the absolute minimum level of politeness, and then I hung up. I stormed back to Lucinda, who hadn't moved. 'That bitch! That dirty little rip-off artist! It was Bertha,' I screamed.

'I thought it might be,' said Lucinda, 'but you're never sure, are you?' she said.

'And did you see how she stole that parking place from me that day?' I sat down and put my finger in Lucinda's cunt. She started to twist her body around them. But I stopped. Too many conflicting emotions were bubbling through me. 'Let's smoke a joint and relax before we begin fucking again,' I said. She shrugged her shoulders. 'O.K.' she said.

We smoked in silence for a while.

She looked good. She had dyed her hair earlier in the day and it now sloped down in wide fuzzy triangles on each side of her head. It was a rich brown. The night before she had stayed up for five hours after I fell asleep, reading, crying, thinking about murder and suicide. It never got too freaky, but it was a bummer for her. I had been dismantled to hear her tell of it. 'Shit,' I thought, 'here comes the messy part. Watching the chick come to pieces.' And I felt an obligation to help her through whatever her changes were, even though I realised that my being there just made matters worse. Classic bind.

189

But by the next day she was gay again, and flirting with the house painter next to the elevator. 'Maybe I should become a dyke,' she said then. 'What do you think, doctor?'

'I think it's a great idea,' I said. 'For one thing, with a woman you could have sex and friendship all wrapped up in one person, something that's almost impossible with most men. And if the two of you had no jealousy, you could still have male lovers when you were in the mood for cock. In fact if the two of you got it together, you could bring men over and put them through enough changes to pay back all the low-life motherfuckers like me you have ever known.'

With that she leaned over and kissed me on the cheek in the most friendly and peaceful manner possible. 'You've never lived with a man, have you?' she said. 'I mean, as a lover.'

'No,' I said.

'Why not?'

I thought about it. 'I was afraid people would think I was queer,' I said, and Lucinda laughed, because the way I said it, it came out like a joke. But what I meant to say was, 'Because *I* might think I was queer.'

Now I took her again, and lodged my body into hers at a thirty degree angle, supporting myself on my hands. At once I had the sense of the openness of her. She shook her head and rolled over, presenting her back to me. I entered her from behind, but with the sense of going in from the front. I realised that a cunt is open from either direction. To a hole, there is no front or back. Any place on the periphery is equal to any other. And there was a nice balance between us. I felt her sucking at my cock with her entire body, and I was aware that she understood how I was digging her reactions as much as my own sensations. It wasn't the glorious sense of *us* which marks the classic transcendental fuck. This was a one-to-one, with a great

190

measure of respect for one another's privacy. After all, the relationship was over. I didn't want to cop out through misrepresenting the significance of the sexual act. Lucinda and I could fuck as deeply as we wanted to, but it must remain clear that this was not the merging of two lovers hustling towards some ultimate come.

It became an oddly homosexual fuck. I screwed her in the cunt the way I would take a man in the arse. And so the criterion became depth of penetration coupled with sensitivity to nuance of touch. I pushed her knees forward so she crouched like a frog, and I fucked her for almost twenty minutes. Much of it was simply loosening up the soil, getting all the stretchy pouch of her cunt supple.

Then I felt her push out, almost as though she were trying to expel me; but it was actually a reaching, a gaping pouting of the cunt lips. I got all the way into her. She was holding nothing back.

I exploded into her inner cunt, and felt my energy penetrating up as far as the third chakra. I fucked her in the spine.

I lost all self-consciousness at the orgasm. It just scraped the balls of heaven clean.

Coming and coming and coming. Each thrust a coming. Each moment an endlessness at the point of edge of coming. Into you now, my lady, so deep into you that I am fucking myself, myself. And the cunt is the secret smile of God.

The ringing phone cascaded in waterfalls of associations and sounds down the blinkings of my waking mind. It was from Janet. 'Please come to the party,' she said. 'Go ahead,' said Lucinda. 'We've fucked. You don't have to try to be noble anymore. Go ahead,' she said as she saw my consternation, 'I'll be all right, really.'

I walked down the garbage-can-lined darkness of Amsterdam Avenue. Puerto Ricans stood under lampposts, cats scurried from car to car like guerrillas seeking cover, and the police patrols stunned the people with their pointed presence. I went into straight paranoid overdrive. I stepped fully into my fear and became bathed in alertness. Suddenly I felt a sweet surge of joy and exultation. Here where a thick stench of brutality turned the concrete black, I was alive, and prowling, and moving from danger to danger through danger, swinging through the physicality of the New York night, from the limb of Lucinda's gurgling mouth and shouting *cunt* to the tree house where the acid monkeys were celebrating the triumph of chaos.

Walking into the house was like stepping into a sauna. Waves of acid vibrations, everyone bright-eyed and frantic for flow, but no one able to manage anything but jagged rhythms. I fell in and out of everyone's basket, surf-riding on the astral plane. The immense potential of humanity staggered me. This was the life force, this was the fantastic energy that is locked in the species, and this is what the dictators of all time have suppressed. This is what the people themselves fear, and so lapse into willing conformity, painting themselves grey, making themselves wrinkled.

I burst through the room like a comet and soared into the backyard. Up above, stars, perpetually mocking my conclusions. I threw myself down into the dirt of Janet's garden and gnawed on the base of a small tree. 'He's fallen on hard times,' said John, standing over me.

Lucinda appeared. 'I decided to come after all. I'm jealous of the dirt.' She sat on my back and I walked off on all fours, she riding me like a child playing horse. 'Very Fellini,' said someone as I moved past.

I crawled past the couples, the fucking couples, the cocksucking cunteating couples, the eternal couples seeking release from completion. The *I Ching* ends with Before Completion. The face of a thin black girl swam before me, her mouth wrapped around a thick white cock, her eyes heavily lidded, as she swooned in that rapturous world between inner and outer experience. I dropped my cock from my zipper and mounted her from behind. Lucinda hit me on the buttocks with a belt. I went on like that. Ululating sisterbrothers emerging into stains and creases in the fabric, the cunning conundrums of our gibbering want.

It was time to leave. She was dressed in velour and gold buckles. We called for quiet as the old man of the mime and his wanton stole past the creaking van of innocent sin. As we passed they fell like phantoms into the concrete reality of the time-speckled departure. And only love was left to wing its widewarped cry into the final night which falls into whimpering awareness of the ultimate of ultimates inexplicably grinning in paroxysms of objective evil dangling from its fragile cord.

Back at the apartment I placed a mirror by the bed and lay back while Lucinda gave me head. She was pure object reflected in the glass, an anonymous source of sensation. I was snuffing out the last twitches of human affection between us. After I left, I didn't want either of us to mourn. It would be better if we died now, in one another's presence.

Her throat went slack and she stopped struggling against my deep slides into her mouth. She gagged, and then gagged again, and finally threw up the cheese and grape juice she had had two hours earlier. It ran down her cheeks and onto the bed. And still I fucked her until I had injected the sperm into her gullet.

It was the day the Arabs blew up jetliners into shining pieces on the desert and men with shotguns were ordered to fly in all the planes.

I pulled out of her mouth and we both lay there breathing to ourselves. A voice rumbled from a window across the alley. Strange realities vibrated. The war would never end.

The purple stain soaked into the sheets. The symbol and the deed ran neck and neck towards the realisation.

XV

What is sex without the games for which it serves as a vehicle?

The next afternoon I ran into Felix, an old lover, in Central Park. We were both doing some uninteresting cruising, and the meeting was coincidental. I felt no real sexual vibration from him, but his presence was not unpleasant, so I walked with him awhile. We talked of past days and mutual acquaintances, and within five minutes I knew I would be going home with him. I found that he offered me a vague sort of comfort. Several years earlier he and his lover-roommate, Donald, had lived in a loft which faced the back window of my apartment. We had flirted across the alley, and soon I was visiting them twice a week for threesomes, and occasionally, when I felt a touch of preference for one of the other, timing my phone calls with when I could see that whoever I wanted to fuck was home.

We had some wine, now, and brought ourselves quickly up to date.

'Donald is leaving for California,' he said.

'Ah,' I said, 'finally going home.'

I saw him then, living behind his sister's bookstore in the shadow of Disneyland, becoming more wan, more fey, until he ultimately settled into type. I found myself taking my shoes off, and as though on signal, Felix got up to draw the curtains. He opened the couch into a bed, and we got undressed, each paying not too much attention to the other. We were entering into an act that was more like a contest, a match of strengths and softness.

He had a small cock, and a wiry body. His fucking was usually frantic, and he would work himself into such a state of surface excitement that he was often incapable of coming. As usual, I began by having him lie back and relax, and then began a long slow journey with my mouth from his navel to his cock. I sucked him a long time, aware of the communion in the touch. But as he began reaching levels of deeper pleasure/pain, feeling simultaneously the throbbing yang of sex and the poignant yin of death, his pelvis began to twitch and soon he was pumping his cock into my mouth with the spastic motions of a dog fucking a bitch. For me it was exciting, until he reached a certain point and his energy began to ebb. We both knew then that he wouldn't come. I became disgruntled, and he got up.

'I think I have a popper,' he said.

He brought it back with an inhalator, holding out to me with a look of painful begging. Obviously he needed me to solve his dilemma. Being an experienced woman, I realised that he was jaded, that is, he got his rocks off on the symbol of what he was doing, not the actuality. My problem was to provide him with an environment in which he could soar into the upper reaches of his fantasy life while remaining unencumbered on the physical plane. But there was a catch. I had to *mean* what I was doing. That was what the drug was for, to give me a temporary rush of energy sufficient to authenticate my act.

I lay back and had him kneel over me, a knee at either

ear. I looked up at his manoeuvred manhood. I broke the ampoule, dropped it into the inhalator, took a whiff, and within seconds began the pulse-pounding ride into the oblivion of surrender. He got hard immediately and began fucking me in the mouth.

'I'm paying off some strange debt,' I thought, 'taking Lucinda's role of the night before and using Felix to play my part.'

There are only five or six good hits on a single charge of the drug, so it was imperative for him to come within the span of time. I looked up at him, he seemed worried. I stepped into my Rumanian role. 'Why don't you masturbate, darling,' I said, 'and use my quivering mouth as your receptacle.' Of course, that seized his fancy.

The rest was quite pleasant. I lay there in a state of somnolent sexuality, buzzing lightly with the energy he jerked off in his desperate need to ejaculate. I sniffed the amyl nitrate from time to time and soared into a private perfumed tent. Finally I heard the sort of grunts associated with male orgasm, and in a moment several thick drops of spunk dribbled onto my tongue.

We had almost nothing to share immediately afterwards, so he went into the kitchen to make some tea. Then we talked about gay liberation, and he promised he would take some nude photos of me. 'I'd like to have a comingout party,' I said. 'Except that everytime I step out of one closet I realise I am moving right into another one. It seems impossible to remain unidentified.'

I left to go to church.

One of the sex trade-journals had advertised a weekly afternoon mass to be held by the American Orthodox Church, a gay congregation. I flashed the possibility of this being the ultimate in camp, with stained-glass windows showing a faggot Christ.

But when I arrived, I found that everyone there was peculiarly straight. They were that particularly odd variety

199

of homosexual that tries to pretend that nothing is amiss. I suspected that the congregation, made up mostly of unattractive people, suffered from a wide range of difficulties, ranging from loneliness to impotence. But who there would understand the sublime sarcasm of that statement?

The priest was a bouncy long-haired and moustached showman of about forty-five with a five-inch aura around his head. He was dressed in all the classic vestments, and garbed himself in the vestibule to the proper prayers. He was assisted by five altar boys, ranging in age from about twenty to forty, performing the usual canopy of activity, swinging incense holders, carrying candles, moving various books and objects around on the altar. One of them had a face of Spanish decadence seen in Velasquez. The choir pew held five young men dressed in slacks and soft sweaters. It was amusing that one did not have to wonder whether any of the choir boys were *that way,* for, presumably, every one of the ninety or hundred people in the church were that way.

I waited through the opening procession, and the first movements of the mass for some spark of put-on, some spirit of celestial goof to lighten the mood, but none appeared. The service was an ancient French rite which had been transcribed into English. We lumbered through the scenario, the hymns sung without comprehension of the meaning of the words, the words from the canon read without elevation of the soul. It was as empty as anything that happens in any of the Catholic or Protestant or Jewish churches every holy day throughout the year.

How odd it was to see all the artifacts and motions which had been engraved in my head as a child, when I, too, took the altar boy trip now going on in this baroque, unintended parody. When I was young, I took it all seriously. To me the priest was an actual representative of God, and when he nodded-out behind his mumbled

200

morning mating call, I used to believe that the bread and wine were literally transformed into the body and blood of Christ. But these people were all adults! Especially the priest. I had nothing but the highest admiration for the theatre which had been mounted, but the actors were taking it all so seriously and the dullness became asphyxiating. History lifted her skirts and smirked as the neo-Christian wing of the gay revolution attempted to breath life into a dead form.

Two moments were heartfelt enough to be moving. At one point, at the consecration of the Host, the altar boy with the ravaged face rang the large church bell by the thick knotted rope which hung by the sacristy. Hearing that golden imperious sound echo off the walls brought sudden tears to my eyes.

And the sermon almost brought me to my feet cheering. As though working out the charade in its most meticulous detail, the priest began with announcements about church business and the formation of a new theatre group. 'We are doing morality plays for Christmas,' he said, and totally missed the irony of his condition. He launched into an inspired rap on the essential worth and dignity of the human being, and included a loving condemnation of the other so-called Christian churches which have no room for their gay brethren. 'We must accept our own beauty,' he said. 'We must realise that being the way we are is part of god's plan for the world. So we do His bidding by being most ourselves. We must stop being ashamed!'

I wanted to jump up and shout, 'Right on brother!' but everything in the church militated against that sort of spontaneous expression. They may have been gay, but Lord, were they *proper*! They took their rejection by the monsters of Western civilisation seriously. And now they were resorting to the quintessential form of that civilisation in an attempt to come to terms with their right to exist fully.

Where the militant gay grouls were strident, these people

whined. It struck me again that the history of mankind is the history of repression, and that large groups of people can be so mocked and threatened from birth that they carry scars of inferiority and fear all their lives. I felt a fine flush of anger, and as has been accompanying that feeling lately, my hand itched for a gun. It seemed that an awful lot of killing would have to take place before the species came to terms with certain basic problems. I felt a strong and animal bond with all the poor bastards in that church who hadn't been allowed to grow into their own kind of people. But as soon as I began thinking about the problem in practical terms, weariness overtook me. Who to kill? How? The enemy was internal as well as external. One couldn't go after a virus with an axe. And I smiled to think of the revolutionaries who would answer my despair by the cry ORGANISE. Organise whom? We are the enemy. And the natural inclination of any group is sooner or later to form an army. War leads to war. There is no hope.

I received communion, and went back to my pew with my head bowed and hands folded. The taste of the wafer sent me into Proustian ecstasies.

Afterwards there was a social hour, with coffee and cookies. I had to keep a strong check on my cynicism, for within minutes after the mass all the celebrants were standing around cruising like crazy. But it was such a guarded and effete flurry of flirtation as to make it almost laughable, except that it made one sad. What were these human beings doing, pretending to plod their way through the fatuousness of organised worship and then coming on with all their selfpity hanging out? It takes great style to pretend not to know what one is doing and make that seem charming.

One tall and lithe cat came up to me and began a standard rap, neither original or despicable, like a Ruy Lopez opening.

'My name's Ken. What's yours?' And then. 'I'm a

musician, what do you do?' And on the eleventh exchange, a surprise move. 'Is there any place in the building we can go?' I looked down. His cock was making a bulge in his pants. He wanted a fast blow job.

I left the scene and went out into Eighth Avenue. Across the street was a familiar building, the City Clinic for Venereal Disease. I wondered whether anyone in the congregation had a sufficient sense of irony to appreciate the juxtaposition of functions.

I called Lucinda but there was no answer, then walked up to John and Janet's and found Jessica. I sank into fucking the way an alcoholic sinks into his bottle.

I did all the required things. I pushed her face with my hand, mashing her mouth and nose out of shape. I slammed into her cunt with full force. I tore at her lips with my teeth. I heard myself grunting and growling.

'Please, please hurt me,' she said.

I was tired and keenly aware of the presence of other people in the house. I couldn't get it together enough to really do it to her, for her to let her have the full hurt. I hooked her knees over my elbows and brought her thighs to either side of her breasts.

'If I don't do it for her, she'll find someone else,' I thought, and the threat of jealousy spurred me on. But as I slashed at her, listening to her cries, and felt my cock grow hotter and her cunt become slack and wet, I felt my anger rise. It was almost always the same with a woman. We begin together and then she sinks into a swoon of rapture, thinking that the depth of her mindlessness is all she ever had to do to please me. I fucked her until four in the morning, changing position, alternately erect and soft, until I could go no further.

'Christ, this is boring.' I thought.

I was suddenly tired of using my cock and caress as a tool to help other people work out the kinks in their sexual fantasies. Stripped of all its therapeutic dynamics, sex was an odd activity. I plunked the sperm into her and collapsed in her arms. She was trembling, seemed frightened. She called my name softly and drew herself closer to me. She said my name again and nestled my face against her chest. I was unsettled by the fragility of her, and waves of tenderness flowed from me to comfort her, to, in some very simple way, *know* her at this moment.

'I'm getting tired,' I thought.

We lay there for a while and soon a current of electricity pulled us together. I began to love her body with my fingers and mouth. She rolled onto her belly, and arched her arse up. I stroked her cunt, and balled my hand into a fist to crush it between her cheeks. Once again she began that high-pitched keening. I inserted one finger, then two, then three. I pushed my hand in past the knuckles and slid the fingers around one another, pummeling the deep inner walls of her cunt.

I slid down so that my face was level with her crotch, and like a mechanic trying to reach some almost inaccessible part of an engine, I probed insistently until I had found all the spots which revved her up to her optimum vibration. She went through one grasping convulsion, and then lay still.

I let my fingers slip out and then began to work with my mouth, licking up the length of her cunt and dipping into her arsehole, rimming her gently and insolently. I buried my face totally between her cheeks and she brought her cunt up, gyrating at her pelvis, rubbing the sticky lips over my forehead and nose and eyes and chin. I took a facial bath in her box.

Then the doorbell rang. I started with fright. It rang again. I became paranoid; I was convinced it was Lucinda. I heard Janet wake John up in the next room. He grumbled and came stumbling past as we lay there in a high-art cunteating posture. He disappeared into the hallway and soon strode past us again on his way to bed. I half sat up,

204

peering into the darkness. I began hallucinating on the shadows. It was Lucinda, carrying a knife, waiting for the right moment to strike.

Jessica turned over and squirmed against me. My cock was numb, but she wanted more. I remembered when Master and Johnson were asked, 'What is the sexual nature of woman?' they answered, 'Insatiable.' She brought her knees to her chest and lay there, cunt agape, waiting for me to put my prick in. I took that absurd appendage in my hand and pulled on its stiffening length. It got hard and I brought it to her cunt, but on meeting that hungry hole, it softened once more. I tried three or four times, once actually rubbing the head of it against her cunt lips. And finally, I gave up.

'It's impossible,' I said, and lay down to go to sleep. Jessica immediately collapsed and curled against me. We fell unconscious breathing into one another's mouths.

I woke up once. John and Janet were fucking. The sound of a slap rang out, and then another. And then eight or ten, very hard, in rapid succession. I could picture her pink buttocks as he crashed the weight and speed of his hand across her arse, WHAP WHAP WHAP.

'Oh God,' she moaned. And then more thrashing noises. He emitted the kind of grunt a person might make upon having a painful splinter pulled out. It was an orgasm of relief.

The next morning Jessica and I fucked once more. It was a grey day as I walked her to the subway. We talked about her former lover, for whom she still had a sense of openness. And about Lucinda, my charge and my sustenance.

'We can stand here after a night of hassle and pleasure and dig one another because we don't live together,' I said. 'It doesn't seem that kind of love is possible any longer. We seem doomed to strip one another very quickly of all our structural necessities, to burn the defensive postures so the energy can flow. But all we accomplish is rubbing one another raw, and destroying what we most admired in one another.'

She looked at me. 'You sure are grim.'

'Just factual,' I said.

I watched the traffic pass. Some four or five million people were beginning another daily round of their fiscal dance, swelling the office buildings and subways and sidewalks with their ordered activity, a vast army of automatons, as conditioned as any nest of worker ants. Freedom was a joke in such circumstances, and love a fairytale. I looked at the pretty girl standing in front of me. There was no way to make her understand my vision.

'The door is shut, locked for a long time, perhaps forever,' I said. 'We're locked in a race between murder and ultimate orgasm. Relationship between a man and a woman is possible only at a distance, even when they are glued to one another's bodies.'

There was a moment of awkwardness. One of our agreements was never to talk in terms of the future. I hedged a bit. 'You'll be at the office every day?' I said. 'One to six every day,' she said. A wordless message flitted between our eyes.

I walked the seven blocks back to Lucinda's house.

206

XVI

The day begins with light stirring and dreams dispersing. Several moments of stunning clarity rush through the entire body and the morning's first tars form as consciousness climbs into the tractor seat to begin another cycle of work. There are flashes of sun-drenched islands and brooding desert plains, whispers of a state of being which transcends the stiffness of the lower back. But plans crop up, and the day's duties present themselves. Then one remembers that one wants to leave the woman one is sleeping next to, or that death is unavoidable, or that the morning paper will provide yet another record of manwomankind's mammoth stupidity. Fantasy crystallises and from its vacuum core a cloud of ambient charges radiate to suffuse all reality with a sense of heightened significance. Then she wakes up, and the first adjustment to another is made, a change that will happen so many times in the crowded city that within an hour one will cease to react to the other humans on the street; they will have no more importance than street signs. Breakfast next, and the necessities perform. Food is ingested, digested, evacuated. Breath continues. The radio, the first look out of the window into the poison air, the sound of car horns, the vibration of mindless commerce. And through all the growing Grand Guignol of life, the leitmotif of sex. Who have I fucked, who am I fucking, who will I fuck? Which cunt? Which cock? Which new spin on the carousel of sensation?

The day descends like a backdrop, a grey gritty lull between the poles of healing unconsciousness. And one by one the persona appear, each to do his or her dance of mortality.

LUCINDA: Her belly began to show the flush of pregnancy. She was to go into the hospital in three days. We both dealt with it as a non-fact, approaching it obliquely, averting our faces.

'Do you want me to drive you to the hospital?' I asked.

'Don't worry about it,' she said.

'I'm not worrying,' I said, my anger flashing. 'I just asked a simple question.' We were doing the kind of manwoman fighting that had been largely absent during the early months of our living together: the woman speaks in terms of her feeling; the man objects to the words she uses; each resents the insensitivity of the other; lines of recalcitrance are drawn; both settle into a lightly venomous silence.

The war will never end.

'It'll be better when it's over,' she said, making the first overture to neutralise the friction. 'You're only guilty before you've committed the crime. Once it's done, you are free of it.'

'That's very Jewish,' I said.

'Except for the baby,' she said. 'Do you ever think of it in there? What it will look like? How it will smile? That's a human being, don't you understand!' Suddenly her eyes were wild and her hair sprang out. She had leapt from calmness to fury without even touching hysteria.

'Bravo,' I said.

'Why are you being so hateful?' she said. We were back

at it again.

It was necessary, then, to fuck her in the arse. The tension between us had reached critical levels, and would have to be discharged. We could either stand there and lacerate one another with words, or we could throw the switch to route the tracks into the sexual realm. I walked up to her and grabbed her sharply by the shoulders. I twisted her torso so that she was simultaneously turned away from me and brought to her knees. I pushed her down onto the floor.

'Don't move,' I said.

I got the K-Y, pulled her housecoat up to reveal her bare arse, and lubricated the hole. The coldness of the act was thrilling, and her submission to it excited me terribly. Of course, it was her excitement also, for she lay there in catatonic bliss waiting to be had.

I fucked her as though she were a corpse, still warm. No life in her, dead, gone beyond any possible recall. Non-existent. Finished. And I fucked her body, grinding the last rub of pleasure ever to be had from her, and with ignominy.

The time until the baby's execution could be counted in hours.

JESSICA: I saw her at the loft where she works as a go-go girl for the city's newest arm of Esalen. We went up to the roof and looked ten floors down to the street of trucks and labouring men. She sat on the ledge.

'I'm afraid of the edge,' I said.

'So am I,' she said, and let one leg dangle into space. My stomach lurched. She leaned over to peer straight down and then turned to me. 'I like you because I can let you be, I have no program for you in my mind. And so you constantly surprise me.'

She looked healthy and neat, and her eyes were filled with a liquid vivacity. I flashed the night before, and remembered how it felt to rub the back of my hands over

211

her entire crotch, beginning between her buttocks and coming up the fur of her cunt to her pubic bone.

'It can't be death you're afraid of,' she said. 'Death is the end, absolutely, you know. How can you fear that?'

'When is your vacation?' I asked.

'Except in America,' she said, 'Here, death is a smiling mortician.'

'We can try Canada,' I said, 'or Morocco.' I frowned. 'You see, the problem is that we have forgotten even what it is like to tell the truth. And sooner or later, we lapse into total ignorance. And then we live our lives by reflex, simple reaction to external stimuli. What if I pushed you, now?'

Her eyes shone. 'Can you imagine the fall? That glorious rush, the knowledge, the *knowledge* of it? And the split-second before hitting. Fully alive, fully alert, never more conscious, and realising the actuality of the end. And then. Nothing?'

Unaccountably I became quite frightened. 'I have to go,' I said.

As we descended I began to wallow in a growing pool of tenderness. I was close to experiencing something like an emotion. I found that I was saying to myself, 'Be careful,' over and over again as I manoeuvred my way down the iron ladder to the fire escape.

'Have you seen *Performance* yet?' I asked.

'No,' she said.

'It's about the best film ever made,' I said. 'It eclipses the truth entirely. And in the darkness it brings about, the unknown is illuminated.'

'What's it about?' she said.

'It's a love story,' I said.

FRANCIS AND BERTHA: I dropped by their place. They reeked of intimacy. As soon as I stepped inside, the vibrations became sharp-edged, pointed, triangular. Their new obsession was a trip to the coast in a few months. 'The four of us can go together,' Francis said, sliding down the wave of his emotional opacity.

'She doesn't like me,' I said pointing at Bertha. 'Can't you fucking understand that yet?' He was silent. 'And I don't want to have any pressure from anyone concerning the scope and variety of my sex life. If you two want to one-to-one it between the sheets, you have my encouragement, but not my recommendation.'

Bertha came up and stood abreast of us. 'You'd better make up your mind whether you want to go with him or not. Because if he goes, I don't.'

Francis looked at us blinking amazement. 'You two can't be serious,' he said.

'Oh, it's real,' I said. 'This is who we are and there's no point in trying to be reasonable about it.'

'But this is insane,' he said.

'Well, it's not like the nuns described it, that's for sure,' said Bertha. The reference to our common nemesis broke the tension and we smiled at one another all around.

'This is the way of it,' I continued. 'It's the same with the three as with two, only more complex, with heavier energies. We're only charges of electricity. We repel one another; we attract one another. We buzz, we flash, we hum, we crackle. And then our ridiculous minds attempt to find some significance in the random patterns we effect. And there is none. We do what we must do by virtue of our structure, and we form our opinions about it in the process. So, go to California with the chick. I'll probably meet you there.'

There was a long moment of silence during which Francis struggled with his heartbeat.

DONALD AND FELIX: Some of the fullest moments of conscious ecstasy have come as I was imbedded between their twin needs, sinking into a violet-black felt passageway and soaring down toward a golden door which opened into an ageless eye which has seen all light.

After our Central Park encounter, Felix had suggested

213

a farewell party for Donald and now we met to begin the evening. It was the first time I had been with them on the street, and they were both dressed in their straight-world clothes, while I hung between them in tight jeans and t-shirt. 'I feel like a trick,' I said, and we all laughed.

Suddenly, the mood changed. All the strangeness we had ever felt with one another disappeared. I looked from one to the other with admiration and affection. These were men with whom I had shared the most intimate of physical experiences, and yet never opened to. And now we were like old friends, teasing. I realised with great relief that the whole world of gay experience was accessible to me. I could make reference and be understood. The area of my personality which is ordinarily kept under wraps burst forth, and I found myself loquacious and bubbly, almost to the point of camp.

'Tonight I'm gay,' I thought. 'I'm being taken for an expensive dinner and am exchanging amusing homosexual small talk down Seventy-first Street. I am in the gay world without having had to join any organisation or make any compromise with my integrity. I am just as much me now as I am at any time of the day in any other circumstances. Doing a homosexual scene doesn't mean being a homosexual.' I felt elated and smiled to myself.

'Well, someone's happy,' said Felix in that arch way.

We enjoyed one another's vibrations in silence for a moment and went in to eat. The food was superb, our table talk was just right, the wine excellent, and the after-dinner coffee and Drambuie faultless.

'I didn't get any poppers,' Felix said.

We got into a cab and headed for a drugstore that will sell them without prescription, but a new man was on duty and he was too frightened to let us have them. Donald called a friend on the East side who was willing to give us six. We took another cab. They lived in a brutally ostentatious highrise with both a doorman and a deskman in the lobby.

'They're a strange couple,' whispered Donald as we went up in the velour elevator. 'Charles, the older man, is a Wallace supporter. Can you believe it?'

'Well, being homosexual doesn't automatically make you a liberal, you know,' Felix said.

'Bitch,' Donald hissed.

'No reason why there shouldn't be gay fascists,' I said.

'But he's against homosexuality,' said Donald. 'I heard him say so. That's insane. He keeps at least two pretty boys as his lovers all the time.'

'America's a crazy country,' I said.

We got the poppers and went back to Felix's place. There was a solid air of expectancy. In the cab I found that I was squirming a little, rubbing my thighs together. How ugly we are when we become insistent about our pleasure. If we got it off, it would be very good. I had had better scenes with other couples, but never as thorough as with these two. I felt oddly cold-blooded.

At the apartment we wasted no time. Within five minutes we had opened the bed and drawn the curtains, taken off our clothes and lit a joint. We relaxed into the marijuana smoke and the warmth of one another's bodies, and a slow easy nodding and fondling began. I let myself slip down the length of Donald's body and in one movement took his half-erect cock into my mouth. Felix raked my torso with his teeth. We were rushing a bit and I wanted to slow the pace down, but Felix took to the heat. He grabbed me hard and pulled me towards him, crushing his mouth against mine. Donald moved down between my legs and prepared to fuck me. I snapped the ampoule of amyl nitrate and sank into that numbing whirring world of wracking sensation.

I moaned as the cock penetrated all the way into me and Felix punished me with his energy. He gnawed at my mouth while Donald began shuddering into my gluteal cunt. Coming so soon! In that strange slant of consciousness so often produced by that drug I sensed that the teeth which ravaged me were embedded in a skull and I flashed that my face was being drawn up into the face of death. As I let myself be sucked up I realised once more how much the ultimate experience of the sexual act is always, for me, the embrace of the grave.

It was a heavy revelation for so early in the orgy.

We fucked for about four hours altogether. During that time we stopped for tea, and once Felix took pictures of Donald and me in a delicate series of poses. In one of them I lay back in what felt like an attitude of abandon while Donald stood over me, six feet tall, long hair and moustache, handsome chiseled features. I was amazed at how cool and light we were with one another, and yet how physically fierce.

Back on the bed. 'Do what you did the other day,' I said to Felix. And he began to pull on his cock, letting the tip of it smash into my lips and onto my tongue. I inhaled more of the aphrodisiac and gummed my way into a soft spastic oblivion. But no matter how hard he tried, he couldn't get it off, and finally he subsided.

He sat down and the three of us stared glumly into space. I was horny. I sat up. 'Well, Donald came, and Felix can't come, and that leaves me.' The two of them looked at me with surprise and then smiled. 'I get to be the director then.' I said. I set the blocking. 'Donald, you go down there and suck my cock. Felix, you can continue trying to come in my mouth, and also supply me with a hit of the popper from time to time. We'll keep doing that until I come, and if you, Felix, come, that's a bonus, but essentially this is my orgasm?'

It was very difficult to keep track of both of them, of my physical state and the state of my fantasies, as well as the general concensus of vibrations in the room, and I kept flashing in and out of one or another aspect of the scene.

216

The single most troublesome awareness during the act was seeing that I wasn't really enjoying the proceedings. I felt as though I were performing a subtle and complex task and that somewhere I was being graded as I would be on a test.

I found myself attempting to get into the consciousness of the other actors. It occurred to me that each of us had come to this point on the basis of some image of expectation of pleasure; this was not an organically spontaneous scene, but rather the reaching after sensation by three jaded sensualists.

This was the final end to Narcissus: finding himself to make love to, and then finding that lovemaking to be unsatisfactory.

And then I came in Donald's mouth.

We lay down for a while and let the jagged vibrations settle.

'What happened?' I said.

'I don't know,' said Donald, 'but I feel like somebody's been stomping me a couple of hours. My mind is sore.'

'I don't know what you two are talking about,' said Felix. He was the only one who hadn't come yet.

'Do you think,' I said to Donald, 'that I can get him to hit me across the buttocks with that gorgeous black belt of his?'

Felix started. 'Do you really want me to hit you?' he asked worriedly.

I lay face down and took another whiff of the popper. Donald straddled my thighs and played with his cock until it got hard again and then sank it between my buttocks and into my hole. It was a relief to be fucked again. He grabbed my hips and pulled my cheeks into his groin. I let myself go slack inside and let him sizzle with all the sensations our friction produced. He came again, moaning. Then Felix crawled onto me and fucked me for fifteen minutes, his cock staying pole-hard but reaching no climax. Unreasonable, I got angry at him and pulled away, leaving him dangling. I was desperately randy. I slid down and took Felix's cock into my mouth, catching him up short just as he was about to begin pouting again. I began to suck him as I never before done in my life. My mouth was a living conscious experience on his flesh. He grabbed his cock and squeezed it. I heard him gasp and just opened my mouth wide. Instantly a wetness of sperm hit my tongue and I swallowed hard. 'I like to swallow it,' I thought, assuming the posture of the wanton who was brought up here to be fucked and used by these two men.

I rolled over and felt the lushness of my body as it touched each of theirs. Donald got on me again, and this time he took me from in front, bringing my knees to my chest. Felix bit very hard into my nipple. I flinched and moaned and drew his head closer to my breast. I sank deeper on Donald's cock and loved every minute of the entire thing. Felix nibbled my cheek. I whispered in his ear. 'You do it,' I said. 'I want the belt.' Donald heard me and his excitement mounted. 'I want the strap on me,' I said, and with that Donald cried out and came inside me for the third time that night.

Felix turned me over. He got off the bed and returned with the belt of leather. I took a pull on a popper and let myself sink into my own sensations.

He began by hitting lightly, and then with sharper strokes. I took both a kinaesthetic and cinematic fix on my condition. As I felt the burning and tingling of the mounting line between tenderness and brutality, I saw the picture from the outside, the thin dark drugged manwoman stretched across the bed as a thick-chested man brought a whip down on the curved buttocks again and again while the third watched with hot-eyed fascination.

The belt came down harder and more frequently. Donald reached down from underneath and began to run his fingers up the crack between the cheeks. His touch was very gentle and I strained to reach it. But as I lifted my

buttocks, the strap came down harder. It was exquisite.
I had to offer my arse to be beaten harder in order to
achieve the delicacy of the caress.

The hand took greater and greater liberties with the
exposure of my desire and finally one finger insinuated itself
into the hole. I gasped for breath. Felix began to hit me
with steady rhythm. I sang in pain and the release of the
moment. I searched for any Freudian demons and laughed
at what I found. Of what interest could any rationalisation
be before the overwhelming reality of the strap, the swish
and the thwack, the quiet fierceness of Felix's
determination, and the depraved dabbling and dallying of
Donald's hand?

'At last,' I thought, 'the belt at last.' And I wondered
whether I would take the final step one day, lying
somewhere, handcuffed and gagged, while an artist of
torture brought my body to its highest tuning.

When I came to, all the activity had stopped. I felt stiff
and sated. The two of them were dozing, one on either
side of me. I got up.

'I really must go,' I said.

'Look me up if you're on the coast,' Donald said.

'Call me,' Felix said.

I got dressed and they walked me to the door.

Out in the street sullen men sat on stoops and drank beer
from cans. Crazies talked to themselves as they walked
down the sidewalks. Police cars glowed on every other
corner.

JOHN AND JANET: Two parasites attempting to suck
one another dry.

'If you loved me, you would come with me,' he said.

'I just want a day by myself,' she said.

'Well, we made this appointment three weeks ago,' he
said.

'Oh, all right, I'll go,' she said.

'Oh don't bother to come if you don't want to,' he said.

'But you know I love you,' she said.
And then I had to leave.

XVII

That aspect of the persona, that 'I', which is most repressed comes, through an ironic transmogrification, to seem our 'deepest' or 'truest' self, that to which we aspire, even though we are unconscious of it. Thus, when we find that we have achieved exactly what we have been striving for, we discover that we have nothing but shit and ashes in our hands.

The following morning began in some miasmal pit. I lay with my eyes closed, awake, for almost an hour after regaining consciousness. I wasn't sleepy, but I could discover no reason to move. My mind was like one of the sixteen-foot pipes that spew garbage into the East River. And I wallowed in the slime and discomfort of it. Then Lucinda got up and went to the bathroom. When she came back I opened my eyes and a look of dense dislike smouldered between us.

'I wonder whether it's a boy or a girl,' she said. 'After the abortion, should I have them look and tell me?'

'I don't want to know,' I said.

'Well, I do,' she said. 'I don't have to tell you.'

She dressed without preparing breakfast. 'I'm going to

223

eat out,' she said, 'do you want to come?'

We found one of those Broadway coffee shops that seem to attract truck drivers and policemen. The eggs tasted as though the chicken that laid them had been fed radioactive dust all their lives. I read the *Times*, a grisly comic book, looking at the photos and snorting at the headlines, then to the bridge column, skipped the book review, and worked up a thin nausea over the insipid commentary of the editorial.

'What did you do last night?' Lucinda asked.

'I had a mini-orgy with a couple of fags I used to know in the Village.'

She smiled with understanding and actual humour. It was the sort of expression which had helped endear her to me. We had become so embroiled in the convolutions of our private drama that we had forgotten to appreciate one another as people. The flash was fleeting but served to illuminate to what degree humanity has lost its ability to exist simply. The earth forms a complete circle about the sun, and to us the importance seems to lie in designating the cycle and calling it a year, while we miss the extraordinary fact of the accomplishment. In that year we wage wars, count profit and loss, persist in our tawdry enterprise, and lose all sight of the awesome breadth of being.

'Why couldn't she have remained independent?' I wondered watching her lips move as she spoke. 'She fell into the role of wife, and I acquiesced out of ignorance and helplessness. I couldn't remain a single man in the arms of a needful woman. And only in those moments when I was again somewhat clear of her, of our scene, could I begin to appreciate her, to enjoy her, to see her as an entity in her own right.' And to step clear involved starting an affair with another woman, a sex marathon with two men, and the possible loss of my friendship with Francis.

Somehow it seems there should be a higher nobility, a

224

greater scope to life than this: diddle around the edges of my frayed and decadent desires.

Back at the apartment we smoked some grass and turned on the television. Nixon was making a speech at Kansas State University as part of the Alf Landon lecture series. There was a great deal of cheering and squealing, the President stomping around the stage with his arms held aloft, a wide-mouthed smile hanging from his ruthless face.

'Thank you, thank you.' He formed the words with his lips but the roar of the crowd drowned his voice. He made downward motions with his hands, indicating that the applause was to stop, and in a few seconds, it did. He came up to the microphone happy. He looked and acted for a moment like Johnny Carson.

'He looks like Johnny Carson,' Lucinda said.

'Johnny Carson can't blow up the world,' I said. '*He* can.'

We both returned our eyes to the screen to look with deadly interest upon this strange man who had become a quasi-dictator in the most powerful nation in the world. A wave of fear washed over us. He told a few jokes. He made a remark about the tie he was wearing. Everyone laughed. Applause broke out again.

'Can it be as infantile as it appears? Are they all really such retarded children?'

Nixon praised Landon, he spoke a few words about how he perceived life ('I've won, and I've lost, and I can tell you this; it feels much better to win.' - cheers), paid off several obscure debts to himself, and went into a rap on democracy.

'In a free society, no one can win all the time, no one can have his way all the time, and no one is right all the time.' And then. 'We cannot respect the rule of law abroad unless we respect the rule of law at home in the United States.'

A three-minute ovation. 'What does that mean?' said

Lucinda.

'It means that the war will continue in Asia and radicals will be totally suppressed here.'

A raucous scream of pain rose from the orderly mob. It was a dissenter. The words were inaudible. Only the tone of the voice, the fear, the confusion, the anger. There is nothing for it. The war will never end.

'Does anyone else understand what is going on? I mean, do they *see*? The *senselessness* of our condition? The mindlessness of the masses and their leaders? Does anyone else realise to what a low estate we've fallen?'

'We must feel nothing but contempt for these radicals, and for anyone who sympathises with them,' the President said.

'Jesus,' said Lucinda, 'Let's get out of the country.'

'Where to, Lucinda? You think it's better anywhere else? Freedom is dead everywhere. The world is dying. You keep forgetting that.'

She screamed once, loud and full. 'No. I don't want to know that,' she yelled, 'I just want to have my baby and live in peace. I don't want much, I really don't want much. Just someplace where there is some peace.' She began sobbing.

XVIII

I lay on my back, sniffing popper's, masturbating. I had no sexual energy left. My cock was bone dry and sore. Yet I had to grab it, to pull at it, to tear the semen from my body. It was a pure act of self-abuse, and I remembered that that was how masturbation used to be called.

I moved from fantasy to fantasy, finding myself close to ejaculation as my images approached degradation. I became a thin sluttish blonde girl addicted to black bodies. I was the personal slave of a sullen brute of a man who used my cunt as a receptacle for all his poison. A friend of his visited the house and as my master left he said, 'You want to use her?' to the other. He turned to look at me, his eyes gleaming. I felt my knees turn to water. I was going to be fucked.

Lucinda slept in the next room. I wondered whether she might hear the sound of my movement, and then didn't care. 'I'm becoming a degenerate,' I thought. And then I wondered by what criteria I was judging myself. Why should this particular bit of behaviour bother me? What were my alternatives? Perhaps I could be dropping fire bombs from an aeroplane. Or reading. Or taking up a hobby. Why not lie back and whack off? As an activity, it ranks close to being the most harmless, and as our Buddhist brethren tell us, harmlessness is the highest virtue.

A trickle of sperm jerked up through the opening and onto my fingers. I looked at it. Just such a load lodged in Lucinda's cunt one night and now a human being was festering in her womb. And soon the salt solution would enter her bloodstream, triggering her uterus into a series of convulsions which would dislodge the troublesome foetus, who was scheduled to ski out on a torrent of blood and tissue.

He will have died with his symbols on.

I was disgusted at myself for thinking contemptuous things about the death of the child, for viewing the entire affair with a sneering witticism. And yet, how could I feel or do other than what I felt and did? Again, it seemed that some value system had insinuated itself into my character, and it was against this that I measured myself.

I got up and went into the kitchen to wipe my hands. I ate a piece of cantaloupe. The cold scrumptious fruit blessed my body as it went down. I felt so much out of contact with the basic realities of life, with the sun, with the air, with the water, with the earth. I was a cell in the body of humankind, and the humankind was dying.

I realised that I had absolutely no idea of how I was supposed to be or how I should behave.

There was nothing else to do, so I went to sleep. Lucinda stirred and woke as I got into bed. She pressed her warm body to me. And I groaned and cursed inwardly as I reached for her.

XIX

Dear Anita,

Last night will remain in my memory as the most perfect evening of its kind that I have ever spent. Many of my sexual gambits are falling away from me these days, and I tick them off as they pass: the last homosexual encounter, the last masturbation, the last literary flirtation. Perhaps, one of these days I shall write THE LAST FUCK in sweat between the breasts of my final woman. Our exchange reminded me that foreplay is by no means inferior to actual penetrating intercourse. And the tension between two narcissists is always exhilarating.

You are a sad human being. The mechanical routine of your life, the compact of helpless emotion between you and your dog, and the growing grimness of old age, are inevitably devestating. but so long as you can convince yourself that awareness saves, you should be able to brazen it through, and die quipping. In all this I see you as a mirror to my own condition, especially in the way your inability to maintain an intimate relationship mimics my own and serves as a model for growing numbers of the species.

I was surprised that we didn't fuck, and found myself smiling as I woke this morning. The contrast this provides to my usual Savonarolian gloom indicated that I must have had a good time last night. But I think that now it will never happen, for having had a chance to think about it, I realise that fucking you would be unbearably tedious.

Picture it. Your Capricornian thrusts challenging my Scorpionic energy. The female in me twittering to the male in you, the stew enlivened by the fact that the woman in me is a lesbian while the man in you is gay. Our minds in a game of speed checkers, leaping over one another to capture and remove. And of course a romp through the dualities, through yielding and firm, through strangeness and familiarity, through sensuality and distance, through fantasy and actuality, through ecstasy and terror, into the eye of orgasm.

May I yawn?

There *is* nothing new under the sun.

How would it have been at first? A long time just kissing, discovering what joyous dances our perfect mouths may make. My full and pouting lips leaning fleshily into your edgily curved wide quivering lips. And then to yearn and strain, to empty and explode, to rise and fall. Until the heat of that energy began to glow in our chests and we crushed our breasts against our breasts and hung in that rare space where for a moment one might believe that love was happening.

And then the rest of it. Fingers, nails, nipples, arseholes, cock, cunt, toes, armpits, bellies, buttocks, kneecaps, and elbows. Rolling around and jockeying for position. Feeling the subtle crescendo of wills meshing. Then to get it in, get it in, now it's in, all the way in, your legs come up and I sink glowingly into you.

Change gears.

You moan and purr. I bite your shoulders. You scrape the skin off my back. For a short while we taste the melting of the shields which guard us. Our auras merge. Genital to genital, mouth to mouth, arms holding loosely tight, we lock to our embrace and rock gently. Small eddies of sheet sensation thrill us together.

'Yes,' you say.

'Yes,' I say.

At which point both of us remember that it will be quite different in the morning and our absolutist conspiracy is another dodge to ward off the horror. In chagrin I pull back and you fall back, and I kneel perpendicular to your torso, turning you over, turning you to the side, passionately technical, taking refuge in control, to blot out that one anguished moment of perception which always sees how solitary and transitory are the transports of the body.

And then, junkies of the soul, we would have to do it again, and again, to reaffirm the deadly vision. And sophisticates that we are, we would eventually bring out the paraphernalia, the props to help us sustain our pain. And then others, as provender for us to feed on. Until the boredom reached such a shattering frequency that we would split violently apart.

And I would say, 'Anita? Oh, yes, we had an *affaire*, but that's all ended now.'

Perhaps the key lies in ceasing to confuse self-destruction with pleasure.

A few weeks before I saw you, I lay in Bosley's arms, he also a Capricorn, but a man, and tall, and black. He caressed me with the most wistful of ironic inflections as I sat on his floor trying to be gay. It was easy to give myself to him, for we could be honest about our despair. Shall I tell you about that fucking? Can you understand how I understand? I have watched women in the throes of orgasm and there is nothing you can experience in the way that I haven't known. The bittersweet of penetration, the relaxation and acceptance, the movement, the joining, the excitement I can never feel when I lie astride a my cock priming a woman's ventures into rapture. And at the finish, feeling as though I had a good massage, and expert and pleasant kneading of my flesh.

And there it is. Evolution's joke. The creation of the sexes. Giving with desire what is taken away by death.

After leaving you I returned to the apartment I share with Lucinda, and fucked her abruptly. For the first time in five months, she wanted to say no. But we both sensed that it was for the last time, so we consented for old time's sake. And we wound up the engine once more, pumping our despair into the night.

Sex is a dead end.

I mailed the letter and felt lighter. Now I had only to deal with the sense of universal despair which permeated my every pore. Walking back from the mailbox I saw an old man on a bench near Central Park. He was doubled over, his arms across his stomach. He looked as though he had been in pain a long time and didn't care any more. The grey drizzle had soaked his matted clothes and little drops of wet had formed in the rim of his dirty hat. On his feet he wore felt slippers, incongruous, probably picked up from the garbage cans in front of the highrise across the way. The air was rotten with exhaust, the passing cars and cabs and buses and trucks exuding the stuff by the millions of gallons. The sky was gunpowder black.

I looked at the faces on the street. I saw masks which told the stories of a million timid tragedies. The hard tight mouths, the quick glittering eyes, the furrowing foreheads, the deadness of expression. Sickness everywhere. Cripples all over.

I passed a bank with its automatons standing glassily

236

behind the cages, and in the window saw a photograph of somewhere in New Mexico, blue sky and clouds, multicoloured mesas. The text stated that the bank would be more than happy to make such a vacation possible for everybody. I thought of the hundreds of thousands who were held in subhuman thrall to the grey dull routines in countless banks across the nation. The giant ritual of money worship for the benifit of the masters of the land.

I flashed the entire horror of the world condition in terms of the implacable greed of the men who owned these banks, who ran the machines of war, who spawned the empires of commerce. The brute fact of human stupidity staggered me. And the situation steadily grew worse.

I realised that the only decent act one could commit in relation to that bank was to totally level it with a massive charge of dynamite.

'Be careful,' I said to myself.

The laws against thought were very close to being enacted. And if I even started thinking about blowing things up they would come and get me. They would put me away. They would kill me.

I walked on. I saw the globe in a single vision, and everywhere grey clouds hung over the land and from them poured down in steady unvarying sheets a cataclysmic rain of pure hatred.

I raised my face and yelled in unholy joy.

Only two of three people even bothered to look up. The rest were dealing with the end of the world in their own way in their own heads, and really couldn't be bothered with someone else's grief.

XX

'Well, are you going to give me the money?'

Lucinda sat propped against the pillows at the foot of the bed and asked for three hundred and fifty dollars, half the price of the abortion. Anger flared through me and I struck out.

'You've got ten years of alimony coming, twenty thousand in the bank, and millionaire parents. And you're asking *me* for money? That would wipe out half of every cent I have in the world.'

'You could at least take responsibility for your half of the pregnancy. Don't stick me with the whole thing.'

'God,' I thought, 'I wish this would end.'

I shouted at her: 'I've taken all the responsibility I can. The money is a separate issue. Can't you see that?'

'I don't feel like being understanding,' she said.

'Fuck it, fuck it, fuck it. I don't want to hear about money. I don't want to hear about problems. I don't want to hear anything.' I grabbed my jacket.

'Where are you going?' She came forward on the bed; she looked worried.

I started for the door.

'Wait,' she said. I stopped. 'I don't want to be alone today.'

I felt like a prick. I went back into the room and sat down at the edge of the bed.

'Can't we just have a day together, just that?' she said. I leaned over and she moved into my arms. The attitude was classic. Corn became the final style. 'I have to go to the doctor's this afternoon,' I said. 'But I can stay until then, and we can have the night together.'

The day went slowly. We ate, read, stared at the ceiling. From time to time I looked out of the window and noted the passage of the hours in terms of the glowing darkness of the day. There was no sun, merely the black and white blanket of pollution that hung a half mile up. I felt myself grow calm, as though the decision to remain together in the space of the apartment obviated the coming split. We entered an almost opiate continuum in which some of our spontaneous liking for one another began to re-form. It became possible for the 'us' to emerge from the 'she' and 'I'. And with that the desire to let the baby be born burst out again, and the hope fell from the centre of Lucinda's eyes whenever she let her control go. Several times the words almost came to my lips, 'Let's leave it all now. Let's find the last place on earth where the poison hasn't reached. Let's try to take care of one another and make a space for our child to grow in.'

Yet each appearance of that thought was met with a ring of destruction, an impulse to find a gun and go out into the streets and begin to kill, to blow holes in the heads of this horrid animal which was rabid with violence and greed. And so I stay suspended in the ultimate posture of impotence: talk.

'Death to the species,' I shouted out loud.

'Oh dear,' said Lucinda, smiling. For she was familiar with, and enjoyed, these tirades. They were something we could share.

'Up with murder and destruction. Don't pay any attention to appearances. They'll smile and they'll seem civil, but they are all conforming fiends, proliferating, bringing more of their kind into the world, making the wars larger, the systems more oppressive, the religions more idiotic.'

'Keep that up and you can run for office,' she said.

'Cruelty is the only way to survive on this godforsaken planet. We've been left on our own and we can't sustain the energy to stay awake. So we kill, and each time we plunge the knife into someone else, it gives us food, it eases our pain. Do you see that? We are imperfectly made. We must do violence to survive.'

'Stop,' she said, 'you are frightening me.'

The vibrations of the room shattered again. 'I'm glad we're killing the baby,' I said, 'it's better off dead.'

I sat down next to Lucinda and spoke gently into her gaze. 'You see what's out there. Institutionalised brutality, from cradle to grave. We've traded the terror of the jungle for the horror of the city. A nation of wage slaves and psychic derelicts stumbling in each day to the choking centres of power to build the latter-day pyramids, to expand the empires of the overlords. They are so demoralised that they have forgotten that such a thing as freedom ever was. I mean real freedom, not that shit the politicians talk about. They beg for crumbs and are happy when the smallest piece of booty falls into their hands.

'It starts with circumcision or baptism or enrolment in some league. From practically the first breath the child is marked with some tattoo to enlist him in the rolls of some imbecile group claiming its separateness from the rest of humanity and the rest of existence. In schools the cry is 'Line up, be quiet' and throughout the vast structure of society the fossil myths fight such duels as to blind all but a very precious few. And the war will never end.

'Lies and lies and lies so dense and interwoven into the

243

very texture of our language that hardly anyone even knows he lies anymore. The masses of people wander in a haze of unperception and a welter of confused emotion, while the intelligentsia become semantic pimps selling the mother tongue as a whore for the rich to use. And all the palliatives fail, all the politics or reform, and the therapies and ideologies and drugs. For there is *no way* out of the hell which increases daily and will soon engulf us entirely. Do you understand that? *No way*.

'Do you think it's sane to attempt to raise a child in such a world?'

I got up and walked to the window. 'Look at the city. It's dying before our eyes, suffocating in its own filth.' I yelled into the street: 'Hooray for filthy air and poisoned water. Hooray for atomic reactors and mountains of garbage.' I spun back to see Lucinda biting her lip.

'Dante G. is only a symbol,' I said to her. 'The real abortion is us. The universe is flushing us out of its system.'

XXI

'Clean all the way down,' he said.

The doctor looked down the entire length of my lower intestinal tract via a hollow two-foot rubber tube which he had inserted, slowly and tentatively, into my arsehole. 'I was about to say "Clean as a whistle",' he said, 'but it seemed indelicate.'

As in most medical situations, we both attempted to pretend that something extremely intimate and sensual wasn't happening. He was exquisitely gentle, with a tender reverence for the body that enriched his consummate expertise. He was like a top mechanic with a really fine engine. As he slid the dildo out I had to exert my will to keep from moaning with pleasure.

'It's a safe bet to assume that the amoebic dysentery has been cleared up,' he said, now sitting across the desk from me. We were dressed; I had put my clothes on and he had rolled his sleeves down. 'We'll do another stool examination in three months and that should wrap it up.'

He stood up and shook my hand. He smiled. My mind teetered. This same man's announcement of the disease some four months earlier had triggered my bout with

247

fidelity and started the trip which was ending with calm despair and kinaesthetic gloom. The end is the same as the beginning, the snake swallows its tail.

I walked back to the apartment through Central Park, relishing the pockets of relatively clean air among the clumps of trees. The rest of Manhattan Island had been stomped flat and covered with cement. It occurred to me that the Indians had lived for almost twenty thousand years on the North American continent and had not left a single mark to mar the beauty of nature. And within a mere three hundred years, the viscious and monumentally insensitive European arrived and turned the entire land into a junk yard, the rivers and lakes into cesspools.

Lucinda was in the bedroom, packing for her stay in the hospital. A man crouched behind the television set.

'He's from Cable TV,' she said.

'It used to be the Fuller Brush man,' I said.

'They were giving a demonstration in the lobby. It only cost six dollars a month.'

'I thought television was supposed to be free,' I said.

'You don't have to get the service,' said the man from behind a tangle of wires. 'Only if you want good reception.'

'It's the logic of madness,' I said to Lucinda. 'Capitalism run amok.'

'At least abortion is legal,' she said.

'It should work fine now,' said the man as he stepped onto the stage of the bedroom floor. He turned the set on. The picture was perfect. He gathered his tools and left, leaving Lucinda and me to watch the end of a very early Bogart film about a ring of Nazis who were trying to lay mines in New York harbour. Peter Lorre played a weird fascist.

We settled in for the evening. We lay on the floor, propped against the mattress, and peered into the tube. Now and then our hands would touch, and we shared a most fleeting pressure, the ghost of an affection that had

248

been mangled by the megamachine and now whimpered behind walls of artificially constructed indifference. My chest was sore from all the aching I had been refusing to allow myself to feel.

She heated up a dish of rice and eggplant left over from two days earlier, as we dipped into the steaming food we both understood that this would probably be our last meal together. We continued to pretend that this was just another evening, though; for, in effect, that's all it was. The emotions were ripcords inside me, and I staggered from moments of crushing loss to giggling euphoria, all within seconds.

We had two bowls of Häagen-Dazs ice cream, and enjoyed them shamelessly, the luxurious seduction of that wet cold flavour temporarily dispelling all other moods and purposes. And then we watched a cast of international stars romp through John Huston's camp on *Casino Royal*.

After all the passion and rationalisation, that is the way the affair ended, with two people stupidly watching television, their faces turned towards the screen like flowers towards the sun, their eyes liquid with guilt; afraid to let one another know their pain, their fear; unable to comfort one another in the face of the great tragedy – the murder of the child.

We walked woodenly through our lines for the rest of the evening, as though we were rehearsing, doing blocking, not actually living the real scene. And then we lay down to sleep.

I had one brief glimpse of the truth of our condition, and then a vast blackness closed over me, as though I were being encased in a huge concrete vault, the thickness of which was the entire breadth of the physical universe. I was ultimately trapped in the toils of existence and in panic my mind raced to the utermost limits of what I could know. All the accumulation of history unrolled before my consciousness, and I perceived that my consciousness was nothing but that accumulation, a dustball of arbitrary structures. As I tripped into sleep I could hear laughter coming from the spaces beyond my prison.

The night was a pool of frightful dreams into which I peered as though through water. Lucinda swam in and out of the field, and I was never sure whether I was seeing the actual woman lying next to me or the crystallisation of a dream. At one moment we held on to each other with all the fullness and freshness of people who have nothing to hold back from one another, as it had once been. And again I sat up, soaked in sweat, and gasped at the speed of time.

Events were out of my grasp. They always had been, but now I didn't even have the illusion of control.

The content of the dreams shifted and refused to stay in focus. But over all was the impression of being beaten with an iron rod, with slow methodical strokes, a punishment that would never stop, no matter whether I slept or woke, day or night. Inside me, always, the club would continue to crush my bones, bruise my flesh.

At six o' clock I got up and walked around. Somewhere behind the dull glow which suffused the sulphurous air outside the window, the sun was shining. I looked over at Lucinda. Her face was wrinkled in pain. I lay back down and fell asleep.

And then Lucinda was shaking me awake.

'You won't be able to visit me today,' she said.

'What?'

'I'll be in isolation.'

I shook my head.

'Don't you know how they're going to do it?' Her eyes were wide and seeing. 'They're going to put in a room with three other women and stick a needle into my arm and let the salt water drip into my bloodstream for ten or twelve hours until the baby suffocates and dies and I begin to abort. And then they'll catch him in a metal pail.'

Hysteria cut though her voice like the whine of a

buzzsaw. I was paralysed. I watched her look at me, waiting. And then she backed out of the room. It took an eternity. I screamed inside my head. But I couldn't break the spell. I fell back unconscious.

I woke up at ten. There was a note on the kitchen table.

> I had written you a long nasty letter – jealous and bitter – but why end that way –
>
> I am sorry about the baby – deeply and forever sorry and sad – I've felt it move and loved it cause it was ours –
>
> I will miss you – five months is a long time – some of it was very good –
>
> I'll be at my mother's apartment for a few days – call if you want –
>
> Thanks for staying around yesterday – it helped

I read it five times, looking at the handwriting, the colour of the ink, the texture of the paper. I tried to feel something. It seemed to me that I should be feeling something.

I scratched around the refrigerator for breakfast, and a rising tide of separateness flooded my soul. For a brief time another human being had crushed through the texture of my alienation and I had felt her as real as myself. Now I was alone again. I was afraid to look at the seconds as they passed.

We began as nomads, we end as monads.

We join the ants and roaches and bees in great unthinking patterns of culture. Or shall we destroy it all? And to whom will it matter?

The hunt is done. We have caught ourselves. Like photographs taken with a flash bulb unawares.

I carefully washed all the dishes and slowly packed what few things I had. I dressed and went into the bathroom. My face in the mirror surprised me, for I looked so normal.

Except for the eyes. Which stared back without question, without wonder, without quarter.

I pissed into the urinal, thinking about what I would do next. It was impossible to stay, and there was no place to go. I flushed the tank with a deliberate twist of the wrist, and watched the yellow water swirl into the base of the bowl on its way to the pipes, into the bowels of the building, under the city street, into the river, and to the wounded and vengeful ocean beyond.

NEXUS BACKLIST

Where a month is marked on the right, this book will not be published until that month in 1994. All books are priced £4.99 unless another price is given.

CONTEMPORARY EROTICA

CONTOURS OF DARKNESS	Marco Vassi		
THE DEVIL'S ADVOCATE	Anonymous		
THE DOMINO TATTOO	Cyrian Amberlake	£4.50	
THE DOMINO ENIGMA	Cyrian Amberlake		
THE DOMINO QUEEN	Cyrian Amberlake		
ELAINE	Stephen Ferris		
EMMA'S SECRET WORLD	Hilary James		
EMMA ENSLAVED	Hilary James		
FALLEN ANGELS	Kendal Grahame		
THE FANTASIES OF JOSEPHINE SCOTT	Josephine Scott		
THE GENTLE DEGENERATES	Marco Vassi		
HEART OF DESIRE	Maria del Rey		
HELEN – A MODERN ODALISQUE	Larry Stern		
HIS MISTRESS'S VOICE	G. C. Scott		Nov
THE HOUSE OF MALDONA	Yolanda Celbridge		Dec
THE INSTITUTE	Maria del Rey		
SISTERHOOD OF THE INSTITUTE	Maria del Rey		Sep
JENNIFER'S INSTRUCTION	Cyrian Amberlake		
MELINDA AND THE MASTER	Susanna Hughes		
MELINDA AND ESMERALDA	Susanna Hughes		
MELINDA AND THE COUNTESS	Susanna Hughes		Dec
MIND BLOWER	Marco Vassi		

EDWARDIAN, VICTORIAN & OLDER EROTICA

ANNIE	Evelyn Culber	
ANNIE AND THE SOCIETY	Evelyn Culber	Oct
BEATRICE	Anonymous	
CHOOSING LOVERS FOR JUSTINE	Aran Ashe	
GARDENS OF DESIRE	Roger Rougiere	
THE LASCIVIOUS MONK	Anonymous	
LURE OF THE MANOR	Barbra Baron	
MAN WITH A MAID 1	Anonymous	
MAN WITH A MAID 2	Anonymous	
MAN WITH A MAID 3	Anonymous	
MEMOIRS OF A CORNISH GOVERNESS	Yolanda Celbridge	
TIME OF HER LIFE	Josephine Scott	
VIOLETTE	Anonymous	

THE JAZZ AGE

BLUE ANGEL DAYS	Margarete von Falkensee	
BLUE ANGEL NIGHTS	Margarete von Falkensee	
BLUE ANGEL SECRETS	Margarete von Falkensee	
CONFESSIONS OF AN ENGLISH MAID	Anonymous	
PLAISIR D'AMOUR	Anne-Marie Villefranche	
FOLIES D'AMOUR	Anne-Marie Villefranche	
JOIE D'AMOUR	Anne-Marie Villefranche	
MYSTERE D'AMOUR	Anne-Marie Villefranche	
SECRETS D'AMOUR	Anne-Marie Villefranche	
SOUVENIR D'AMOUR	Anne-Marie Villefranche	
WAR IN HIGH HEELS	Piers Falconer	

SAMPLERS & COLLECTIONS

EROTICON 1	ed. J-P Spencer	
EROTICON 2	ed. J-P Spencer	
EROTICON 3	ed. J-P Spencer	
EROTICON 4	ed. J-P Spencer	
NEW EROTICA 1	ed. Esme Ombreux	
NEW EROTICA 2	ed. Esme Ombreux	
THE FIESTA LETTERS	ed. Chris Lloyd	£4.50

Please send me the books I have ticked above.

Name ....
Address ....
....
.... Post code ....

Send to: **Cash Sales, Nexus Books, 332 Ladbroke Grove, London W10 5AH**

Please enclose a cheque or postal order, made payable to **Nexus Books**, to the value of the books you have ordered plus postage and packing costs as follows:

UK and BFPO – £1.00 for the first book, 50p for the second book, and 30p for each subsequent book to a maximum of £3.00;

Overseas (including Republic of Ireland) – £2.00 for the first book, £1.00 for the second book, and 50p for each subsequent book.

If you would prefer to pay by VISA or ACCESS/MASTERCARD, please write your card number here:

Please allow up to 28 days for delivery

— — — —   — — — —   — — — —   — — — —

Signature: _____